More Praise for *Beheld*

"A compelling new novel by TaraShea Nesbit, author of *The Wives of Los Alamos*, explores not only the dangers the first colonists confronted on arrival, but those they brought with them . . . *Beheld* disrupts expectation to render the pulsing messy lives of those too often calcified in myth." —*USA Today*

"I have been waiting for this book. But I'm not alone. There has been a sort of impatience and delicious anticipation felt by those waiting to be inside TaraShea Nesbit's much talked about *Beheld*." —Sarah Jessica Parker, via Instagram

. "There is a contradiction underpinning the whole project of English imperialism, and Nesbit flags it perfectly . . . The novel is most successful where it allows itself to stray from historical fact and plot—to invent and to play with language, to give itself imaginative time and space. Nesbit is brilliant in those moments, and captures a paradox of historical writing—that it's in the invention and improvisation that the past feels most pressing and most real." —*The New York Times Book Review*

"In a gripping retelling of the Plymouth colony's first murder, we finally hear the voices of women—and they speak an unvarnished truth that turns history on its pointy-hatted head. Truly a riveting read." —Helen Simonson, author of *Major Pettigrew's Last Stand* and *The Summer Before the War*

"TaraShea Nesbit's puritans are passionate and vengeful and entrancing. Part mystery, part love story, beautifully told and meticulously researched, *Beheld* reanimates and complicates the mythologies of America's earliest settlers. I was sad when it ended." —Anton DiSclafani, author of *The Yonahlossee Riding Camp for Girls*

"*Beheld* breathes fresh life into a world grown still and murky beneath the scrim of legend—rife with intrigue, fractured by difference, marked by violence, and full of haunting images. With gorgeous, period-inflected prose, Nesbit takes us back to the earliest days of New England to look through the eyes and over the shoulders of historical characters both remembered and not. I read it at a gallop. What a marvel this novel is." —Laird Hunt, author of *In the House in the Dark of the Woods*

"I read TaraShea Nesbit's *Beheld* months ago, and it's one of those novels that has stayed with me—in the best way." —Tina Jordan, *New York Times Book Review* deputy editor, via Twitter

"Nesbit . . . cleverly recasts pilgrim history in this deeply enjoyable novel . . . Capturing the alternating voices of the haves (the Bradfords, Newcomen) and the have-nots (the Billingtons), Nesbit's lush prose adds texture to stories of the colony's women, and her deep immersion in primary sources adds complexity to the historical record." —*Publishers Weekly* (starred review)

"Nesbit joins other writers of colonial life, such as Nathaniel Hawthorne himself, to show how easily hypocrisy and the puritan faith merged in society. Eleanor has her own scarlet letter because of her marriage, her social status, and her outspoken bravery." —*Washington Independent Review of Books*

"The novel is a gripping read propelled by vibrant characterization, and an engrossing take on the Plymouth colony and America's first murder." —*Historical Novel Society*

"*Beheld* is a thrilling, class-conscious take on the narrative of Plymouth that introduces marginalized voices whose stories are rarely told." —*BookBrowse* (four stars out of five)

"Restoring women's voices, primarily through Alice and Eleanor, adds a new and welcome dimension to our history, made more vivid by solid research and clear, concise prose. In Nesbit's hands, history once again comes alive." —*Booklist*

"Nesbit brilliantly captures the wrath between the classes and the irony of coming to a country in pursuit of religious freedom only to have the sanctimonious puritans circumscribe the rights of the Anglicans." —*Publishers Weekly*

"Nesbit's novel has all the juicy sex, lies, and violence of a prestige Netflix drama and shines surprising light on the earliest years of America, massive warts and all. A dramatic look at the pilgrims as seen through women's eyes." —*Kirkus Reviews*

"Nesbit tells this story of conflict and contradiction in alternating chapters from both the empowered and the powerless. The voices of the women are especially strong, particularly Elizabeth, whose friendships and reminiscences of the colony's

Beheld

earlier days offer insight about the women of the plantation . . .
Land ownership, religious observation and differing accounts of
events all play their part in this clever, insightful novel that digs
deeply into our country's conflicted origins." —*BookPage*

"Nesbit's empathy is as evident and important here as her
commitment to accuracy . . . Reading historical fiction with a
balanced combination of accuracy and emotion can approach
reading a letter or a diary from the time. Such fiction can also
offer intentional, carefully crafted drama and, in Nesbit's case,
beautiful prose. *Beheld* will engage readers who seek out historical fiction, and others who enjoy voice-driven psychological
drama." —*Fiction Writers Review*

"Nesbit does a wonderful job of showing how a mind can
be skewed to a certain train of thought." —*Bowling Green
Daily News*

"This is one of those gaspy tales that can hold you enthralled
until it's time to shock you good, and if you need something
different, find it. Indeed, *Beheld* is a book you must have."
—The Bookworm Sez

"Get ready for what the ladies of Plymouth have to say."
—Paperback Paris

"The author's nuanced and careful attention to the inner
lives of women and underdogs is notable. It represents one
of the best impulses in contemporary historical fiction."
—*The Christian Century*

Beheld

A Novel

TaraShea Nesbit

BLOOMSBURY PUBLISHING
NEW YORK · LONDON · OXFORD · NEW DELHI · SYDNEY

BLOOMSBURY PUBLISHING
Bloomsbury Publishing Inc.
1385 Broadway, New York, NY 10018, USA

BLOOMSBURY, BLOOMSBURY PUBLISHING, and the Diana logo
are trademarks of Bloomsbury Publishing Plc

First published in the United States 2020
This edition published 2021

ISBN: HB: 978-1-63557-322-0; PB: 978-1-63557-655-9;
EBOOK: 978-1-63557-323-7

LIBRARY OF CONGRESS CATALOGING-IN-PUBLICATION DATA IS AVAILABLE

2 4 6 8 10 9 7 5 3 1

Typeset by Westchester Publishing Services
Printed and bound in the U.S.A.

To find out more about our authors and books visit
www.bloomsbury.com
and sign up for our newsletters.

Bloomsbury books may be purchased for business or promotional use. For
information on bulk purchases please contact Macmillan Corporate and
Premium Sales Department at specialmarkets@macmillan.com.

In memory of my great-grandmother, Fonda Davis

Beheld

1630

New Plymouth

Part One

Alice Bradford

We thought ourselves a murderless colony. In God's good favor, we created a place on a hill overlooking the sea, in the direction from which we came. For a while, God's favor seemed possible. But it pleased Him to have other plans.

I remember that day, in the year of our Lord sixteen hundred and thirty, that the first colonist was murdered. We were divided, as we had been from the beginning— half of the colonists were congregants striving to live as God intended. And the other half? Well, they were why we took care to mend the fences.

It was August, the month of promises fulfilled or never realized. Our harvest had been bountiful: acres of nearly ripe corn, beans, and squash. I had three living children with me in Plymouth. William the younger was six. Mercy was three, already feeding herself porridge, and gentle with the newborn Joseph, when reminded. My two eldest were still in Holland. At forty years of age, I was for the final time a new mother. Joseph, two weeks old, newly whelped. I was blessed to have so many healthy children.

My husband saw the ship's arrival first. He lifted the oiled cloth on the window and said, *They'll be here by supper.* The newcomers were at least a week past due.

Young William followed his father in nearly all ways, including, that morning, climbing up on a chair to see out the window, though he, unbalanced, fell backward. His skull knocked against the floor. I jumped and gave the baby to his father. Everything could have been a sign of what was to come.

I took young William in my arms. He was a clumsy child but recovered quickly, and soon asked to be excused to milk the heifer. It was one of the few chores he enjoyed doing, though he had heard *God is always watching* enough not to stray too often from his tasks.

Downward to the sea was the shore and a single ship that at this distance looked so quiet, one could think of it as a peaceful sign or as a menace. The ocean rolled toward us. Surrounding Plymouth was the palisade and past the palisade, the wolves. Wolves, so close to resembling our companions, but not of our kinship. Killing our swine and our cows. What swine and cows we had left foraged and trampled on the Wampanoag's crops. We erected more fences. We affirmed we were not at fault. I calculated, incorrectly, that the ship would be here before lunch.

John Billington

J ohn Billington loved mornings. He loved waking
before his wife and sons, before the human world
woke. If he stirred before them, he thought it already a
day blessed by God. When the boys were young—for
seven years at least—there had not been a morning like this.
Now, his eldest, John the younger, was two years dead, in
a grave behind his house. His youngest, Francis, was in bed
with his mother.

John Billington heard the *ee-oh-lay* of thrush. He imagined what trees the birds were on, what fences. Ten, then
twenty, the numbers swelling, growing louder, until there
seemed to be a symphony. He smiled large enough to
reveal his rotting front tooth. His wife and son slept
through the noise. Astonishing it was, to hear the low hum
in the background of your life brought forth to a crescendo.
At fifty years of age, he knew the world was painful, but
also beautiful.

Behind the sound of birds, he heard his goat, Mary, opening herself up for her infant. Two weeks earlier she bore three babies. The runt, a male, was the only to survive. He suckled greedily at the teat.

The birds were startling in their shrill calls to one another. Though perhaps this was not a happy sound at all, but instead rivalry. The birdsong came to a halt. He did not hear their wings flapping in the wind. It was as if they saw something and, in fear, kept quiet. He could no longer hear the goats, either. Had sound itself ceased?

John Billington tiptoed from his bed to the door, opened it only enough to slip out. He was a slender man, often preferring drink to food, and the door made little sound.

Outside, nothing was amiss. His house was still directly across from Governor Bradford's. He was still at the crossroads betwixt the wide road that ran east–west, from the ocean to the meetinghouse, and the road that ran north–south. He was still in the last place he wished to be: at the center of it all, so the puritan hypocrites could place their watchful eyes upon him. These puritans kept their enemies close.

Why were they hypocrites? The reasons were numerous, but on this morning John Billington was most concerned thus: that they forbid commoners such as himself from trading with the Wampanoag Indians while they did so freely. As if the Indians were murderers, when in fact the only ones near Plymouth who had murdered were

Captain Standish and his militia, the proof of which—Wituwamat's head on a stake—was erected atop the roof of the meetinghouse. In pamphlets the puritans called the Indians idle, unable to help themselves, poor farmers who left the land desolate and therefore ready for the English. But it was Squanto who had shown them how to fertilize the sandy, shallow soil with fish; it was the Wampanoag Indians who gave them seeds to grow squash, corn, and beans. It was the knowledge of the Wampanoag women, planting in their own fields, that they had, in the beginning, relied upon. All things Governor Bradford would never put in writing. A disgrace that the hypocrites called themselves godly men and lied thus to get what it was they wanted: profit. John Billington had every right to trade with them.

The birds were gone. Who or what had provoked them? Had Billington had too much ale last evening? No, two pints only, though he had hoped for more.

A lone colonist walked up the hill toward the meetinghouse. A man whose face and gait he did not recognize. Beyond him, on the water, at a distance Billington could barely see, was a ship full of passengers, passengers sold on lies about what awaited them. His own experience on the *Mayflower*, though ten years past, was palpable. He had been the tenth person to step off the ship. He should be considered an elder. But the leaders of Plymouth would never recognize him as such. Those like him—the former and current indentured servants, the commoners—treated him with deference. There were three hundred people in Plymouth now. Some were unfamiliar to him. But he'd been here long enough to have many familiars whom he wished were strangers.

As if Billington had conjured him with his thoughts, Governor Bradford stepped out of his house. Billington looked away, but was not quick enough. Governor Bradford tipped his hat.

The elders would never be his friends.

Ten years before, when the hypocrites' ship, the *Speedwell*, had sprung a leak—twice—they demanded a place on the already-crowded *Mayflower*. Bradford, who was then just a man with self-righteousness and an inheritance, asked John Billington to move his family's place from the center of the ship to the side, where, during a storm, the water might run.

You'd have me sleep with the gunpowder? Billington had said.

Rather than turn back to Holland, whence they came, the puritans had persisted in adding themselves to the *Mayflower*. Billington knew they were a people who believed in God's back parts—that God was ever present even when not visible. They believed in signs, as he did, so he spoke to them thus.

Perhaps the leaking Speedwell *is a sign, Master Bradford?*

William Bradford turned.

A sign you should go back to Holland. Perhaps God does not wish you to see the New World.

Profane, Bradford said, rather loudly, to his first wife, Dorothy—rest her soul—which was not for Dorothy at all, but for Billington. That was the first of many conflicts betwixt them.

Billington wondered what allies and what foes might be aboard this approaching ship.

It was not he, John Billington, nor his kind, who supported Bradford as governor. Billington had arrived as an indentured servant and as such was not even permitted to vote. Had the servants had a vote, Billington's people would have been in the majority and Billington's kind would have led. But no, he knew, they never would. They never did.

John Billington had not been brought up with an inheritance, as Bradford, Brewster, and Carver were, as many of these hypocrites were, though they complained that Holland did not offer them enough. Being poor did not make him, John Billington, profane. Profanity was a man who preached God's way and acted against it. Profanity was forbidding baptism and the celebration of Christmas, as these puritans did.

Plymouth was the England that John Billington had tried to escape, just under a different name. Instead of King James, there was Governor Bradford and his hired soldier, Myles Standish.

Billington let the chickens out of their coop. They rushed toward him, eager for scraps, but he had left the carrots and corn in the house. He lunged. *Shoo.*

Dear God, he thought. *Those birds. What sign could this be?* A voice came to him, as it did on occasion. The voice may have been his own, or may have been his ancestors, or may have been God. But whenever it spoke, he listened. *Today all will appear the same, but something will not be.*

Alice Bradford

I sat back in the rocking chair and nursed Joseph.

William tied his boots and said, *Pay a visit to Mistress Billington? See to it that she understands the severity of her husband's transgression.*

I nodded, but I was in turmoil. How little I knew when first I agreed to be a governor's wife.

I was to warn Mistress Billington that her husband's letter to the colony's investors, complaining of his ill treatment, was known to my husband, and in the future her husband would be punished. Master Billington, the Judas amongst us, *the elder of the most profane family*, as William often said, had told our investors that more than half those aboard the *Mayflower* had perished that first winter—a fact known—but also wrote that the land was barren, and that the beaver had moved farther north at our scent. His letter claimed that our one hired soldier, Myles Standish, was cruel and ill suited, and created unnecessary tension with the Indians. That more men were sick than working. That Weston, the liaison betwixt ourselves and the investors, was a thief and a liar, and had taken his family to Plymouth on false pretenses.

We were to be in Virginia, Billington railed. *And he knowingly took us north, outside of jurisdiction. It was their plan all along. These hypocrites are thieves.*

I confess that William's earlier report of the land here being an embarrassment of riches was a bit of speculation. He began writing before he'd arrived ashore. Nevertheless, we were presently thriving.

Beaver pelts, more fish than one can net, and if you have harpooning equipment, whale oil to live your life on, William wrote, advertising our colony in a pamphlet distributed throughout England, hoping for more colonists to join us.

Billington signed his letter to the investors as *The Ill-Treated Servant*.

What is this? the investors had asked William in a recent letter, about Billington's claims.

William's letter back to investors—now sitting on his desk, to be sent with this incoming ship's departure—assured them of Plymouth's fecundity and reminded them of the trouble Master Billington had caused us since first he stepped aboard the *Mayflower* with his wife and two ill-behaved boys, toothless and shoving their hands in the casks of gunpowder.

God tests, I'd say, when Billington interrupted my husband's dinner speech with complaints.

But William always replied, *And, so, too, doth God punish.*

The Billington boys had shot their father's musket and nearly set fire to the *Mayflower* ten years ago, and when John the younger had wandered off into the woods and was returned a month later by the Nauset, I am not the only mother who wished he would have stayed away. His mother slapped his face and called him an ungrateful twit. I imagine the Indians were glad to be rid of him.

Of all the regrets William had about his negotiations with the investors, at the top of his list was that John Billington was allowed to sign up as an indentured servant, bring his family, and board the *Mayflower.*

My husband did not want Master Billington at tonight's dinner and had taken an approach on two fronts. Captain Standish would tell him there was no room, and I would warn his wife. He would be squeezed from both sides, until he was forced to change his ways, or leave. That was the plan, anyway.

The letter from our investors—to whom we still owed a significant sum—said a representative was on the *Gifte*, that ship out at sea. They were coming to celebrate our great harvest.

What wonderful news, I had said.

But William scowled.

No businessman says what he means. They are coming to oversee us because Billington has stirred in them doubt about my ability to lead.

There was still so much for me to learn. William was learning, too, as he went along. Almost nine years into his role as governor was mere infancy in politics.

To be a successful colony, to pay off our debts, to be free of England, we needed a good reputation. If Master Billington's letter got out, if someone published it as a pamphlet—and oh, how the lascivious, gossip-mongering Londoners would revel in our failure, *the hypocrites, the puritans,* as they would say, mocking us—at stake could be our colony, our future, our children's lives, our freedom.

How to contain the fire of Master Billington so we would not lose good colonists and how to present our colony to the newcomers in a good light were the main tasks for William and me on the day the new colonists arrived. Of course, it would not be hard, I had thought. We were a colony fashioned in God's favor.

William stood behind me and placed his hand atop my head. I looked up at him. He smiled at Joseph.

He kissed my neck. I felt the warmth of his lips, his breath on my earlobe. A soft kiss at my collarbone. He slipped his hand upon my bosom. I did not welcome this as much as God would wish it. As desirous of him as I was, I never was when the children were close.

But other times, yes. My husband's mouth betwixt my legs last evening.

If Eleanor presses you, prithee tell her I have done all that I can. But I might not be so generous in the future.

I was not accustomed yet to using this kind of persuasion. It was unspoken of my role, but I knew it: to tell William what the people felt and to persuade the other half of the colony's citizens—the women—that my husband made the right decisions. Amongst my kind, I liked this work. It gave me purpose. But to go to one of our former servants and try to convince her of something? I did not want that task, nor did I think I could achieve it.

I will, I said. It was the quickest way to assure him I would speak with Eleanor. Saying more might further reveal my turmoil.

Joseph slept against my chest, a warm dumpling. I relaxed and thought of all we women still needed to do to get ready for the new colonists' dinner: more pies to bake, more bread to finish, more stew to cook, tables to set, and so forth. I could hear William the younger following his father up the hill, the goat's bell jingling alongside him, on his way to the field. The same field that would be made bloody by the day's later violence.

Until the ship docked, my husband would count beaver pelts, hammer fences, and curse at inanimate objects, as was his way. The children would try to get out of the work it was their duty to do. I cajoled them with threats—*God is watching!*—but that often failed. Instead, I'd make a game of it. *Who can find the most stones?* I'd say to get them to prepare the ground for crops. I'd toss a cow's knucklebone in the garden and ask them to hunt for treasures. But games only go so far. For the rest, there was the guidance of Scripture: *He that spareth his rod hateth his son; But he that loveth him chasteneth him betime.*

I stepped outside.

The two women I called my friends were already in their gardens, pulling weeds and plucking herbs. Our home was where the two main roads of our colony intersected, making an elongated cross. Broad Street ran down a gentle hill east to the sea and west up the hill to the meetinghouse. Our second street ran north and south, the entire length of our walled-in colony. The palisade—a wooden fence with sharpened pales around the interior of the colony— was eight feet high and kept our colony safe. To step into the outer fields, one had to pass the guards.

A breeze blew in light and cool. I watched the wind flutter the leaves and make mottled shadows on the houses. The birds flew overhead, their sounds loud and chattery. All, I affirmed, would be as God intended.

I glanced at my neighbor, Susanna, round at the belly, nearing the end of her pregnancy, and across from her, Elizabeth, hands in the dirt. Both women had survived the *Mayflower*'s journey. They were the only two women left from that ship aside from Eleanor Billington. My husband's first wife, Dorothy, my own dearest consort, was on the *Mayflower*, but she did not survive it, and I was beckoned by William one year later. She slipped, the ship's second mate said. I have long wondered otherwise. My husband and I do not speak of it.

Where our fences met, Susanna leaned.

And I told her help was needed at home, first.

That was Susanna, always Susanna, complaining about her servants. She was a fair woman, blond hair, with freckles on her cheeks you could see only if you were close enough to kiss her.

I wondered who it was they were talking about, but then I remembered that I did not really care. Rather, I was feeling the care from the group, which always conspires to swirl others up into its persuasions. But since I'd become the governor's wife, the women told me less. I was the earpiece to authority. Despite our community's higher plans, every place has rank. The world swings back to it, because no man or woman is as good or godly as he or she wishes to be.

Who's that? I asked, tempted.

Susanna opened her mouth to say it, when the three of us heard a front door slam. We turned.

Susanna, what is this?

It was her husband calling from the threshold, pointing to a wreath of flowers on their door. Susanna was nine years into her marriage with Edward Winslow, an elder of the colony.

Daisies, Good Husband, Susanna said and turned back toward her friends.

Master Winslow was testy when there were newcomers. Though it was he and my husband who advertised the fertility and abundance of New Plymouth, there were always newcomers who asked for more than what God granted. Before each new arrival Susanna's husband reminded us of the new colonists' false beliefs, saying, *They come here expecting beer to flow from the brook, the woods to be a butcher shop, and the lake to be a fishmonger's stall.* It was true. *Bring us not your butter-fingered, your sweet-toothed, your faint-hearted,* I thought. When a new ship docked, I was quick to assess who might give cause for concern. And I often guessed correctly.

Master Winslow admonished Susanna for puncturing the wood of the door and wasting the metal of a nail. He continued grumbling as he walked up the hill to the men working on two half-built roofs. He spoke loud enough for his wife to register the grumbling, but not loud enough to elevate his annoyance into an argument, as is common with husbands.

Adornment is a vanity, Susanna said to us with a smile.

It was the familiar refrain our husbands sang against our homemaking.

Elizabeth raised her eyebrows.

What? He has his gold tassels. I have my wreaths.

❁

The arrival of a ship of new colonists had us looking more often in puddles, glancing at our own image, wondering

what the newcomers would see. It had been a whole
season since we had expected new people. In all of us, I
saw, there was a slightly turned or upright posture, the
awareness that soon, someone new would see us. How
would we look?

The cuts of our clothing were practical, efficient, and
unadorned, but in color we were never modest. Susanna
wore a dress the color of corn silk. Elizabeth wore russet.
I favored green, to complement my eyes.

But I was a plain woman. Even as a child I had dark
fine hair on my face, for which other girls teased, but I did
not pluck, following my mother's warning.

Italian as a fork, one shopkeeper in Leiden always said
when I walked by, despite my many times of saying, *I am
English, sir*, in Dutch.

In Amsterdam, you could be from anywhere. The
older I got the more vain I became, consumed by it before
marriage, regretful of it by motherhood. I would not
become a woman worried about appearances, staring too
long at her reflection. We were trying to be in God's
good favor, and whatever was fashionable was lowly and
earthly. Beauty was a vanity, an earthly vanity, which is
why the royalty spent their time upon it. That was not us,
I kept telling myself, but privately I believed it was far easier
to be less vain when you were beautiful. As Dorothy was.

I felt a pinch, lifted up my skirt, and slapped my calf.
The first fat mosquito of the day, black and dead against
my leg, with my own blood oozing out. A welt already

forming. There was nothing like this in Holland, nor in my birthplace of Wrington, England, two places mostly free of anything that would bite or sting, except the people.

When colonists made the mistake of complaining of the humming bloodsuckers aloud, my husband said, *If you cannot tolerate a small insect, you do not deserve what God has given us. People who cannot endure the bite of a mosquito are too delicate and unfit to begin new plantations and colonies.*

William expected from others the austerity and work ethic he imposed on himself. It was one of many signs that he was of God's chosen, that he would be saved in the most perilous of situations. Whether encountering the Indians for the first time or making his own path from orphan to governor. And because he felt chosen to me, he also felt prescient. As if any lie I were to tell, or half-truth, would be immediately seen by God *and* William. I was not as austere as he was, and each time I wished for more than he did, I tried to redouble my efforts. I wanted more, often.

Nearly everything had flourished that summer except peas, which every year we blamed on poor timing of the planting, but nothing seemed to work. I missed peas. This season had been better than the last six that I was privy to, but no one knew what the investors would say. Investors always wanted more.

My sister lived in Plymouth, which was a comfort, but she had traveled to Salem with her husband.

We heard another door and looked outward. Across the way, Eleanor Billington had stepped out of her house.

Eleanor Billington, black curly hair loosely tied back and falling forward onto her shoulders. She wore a bosom-bursting dress, free at the waist but tight at the chest. She darted to her firewood. An urgency, there was, not to stare, for the U-shaped cut that revealed her bosom. She picked up wood and went back inside before Susanna could give commentary.

Susanna nodded her head, as if to say, *See, this is the woman who is not doing her share.* As if God was making now her presence known.

What do you think will happen first? Her husband killed or kicked out of the colony? said Susanna.

I told her that was a terrible thing to say. Her son, who had passed just two years prior. But God doth punish.

So many people died that first winter in Plymouth, but like the most pernicious weeds, the Billingtons had survived. Why did God spare them? Thrice William had threatened to kick the Billingtons out of the colony and thrice Eleanor saved her family from her husband's belligerence.

I bit my forefinger. Again it bled and again I admonished myself. We never intended to have Eleanor Billington's kind amongst us. The murmur was they were the sign of Satan's presence.

And yet, there was something about her I liked, something I could not name that drew my interest, despite how publicly I stood beside my husband.

Of the devil's presence? Methinks not, said Susanna.

She scurries like a rat, dothn't she? Elizabeth said.

A scrawny little rat, said Susanna.

Behind our backs, our servants whispered, too. When they thought we could not hear them, at the trough, milking cows, at the ovens, they called us puritans and hypocrites, they called us sticklers and precisionists. We wanted to reduce the clergy's hold on the Bible and they said we wanted to take the *merry* out of Merry England. But this was not England, this was Plymouth, a land designed in God's good favor. I had not anticipated that to be amongst our Anglican servants—most of whom were commoners from England—was to be again amongst those who hated us.

But we had nearly gained self-sufficiency. There were only a few more payments left to the London bankers. We could lead in the ways God preferred. No icons of God, whose face no one had ever seen. No alms paid for misdeeds, no unnecessary celebrations, like Christmas, which had no scriptural history. Free, we would be, from most earthly trappings.

Eleanor Billington

I 'm leaving my house, right, John and our son already out in the fields. I'm getting the logs, as one doth, minding my own, when those three steely faces turned to me. Oh, their chaste little bosoms, their pious little smiles. Women who think they are better than I. Than us, the servants. But we weren't their servants, nay, not any longer. One year out of indentured servitude but watching them look at me, you'd never know it.

I took enough of those glances in London—I shan't be needing them now, mistresses, I yelled across the gardens.

Alice, the governor's wife, covered her chest. Susanna put her hand on her hip. Elizabeth went back to her weed pulling. Revelry, it was, to rile them.

Sing for your supper, that is what my mum did, sang for her bloody supper, and I did what I had to, did I not? To pay Weston for this journey. Given how we lived on the *Mayflower*, on the wet ship floor with the rats nibbling our toes, he should have paid us. When my feet first fell upon this land, I had in mind to return to the ship's Master and say, *Take me back. This was not the ticket I purchased.* We agreed to seven years of labor with respectable, ordinary English people. We agreed to seven years of servitude in Virginia, not Plymouth. But oh no, no, no, William Bradford had an answer. My kind, my common kind, we are never given what we are promised.

It made our men sour, to put up with what they did, in England and in Plymouth. The chimney sweep boys, the Thames fetchers, when every man you walked by in London was a man thinking he could buy whatever he wished for—a biscuit, a black hen, a backside. And they could, could they not? That was these puritans. You couldn't say that word to their faces though. They claimed it was slanderous. It wasn't. It was truth. I knew as soon as they put their self-righteous boots on the *Mayflower* they would be trouble. Asking us to quiet our singing, scowling when we passed the time by dancing.

They would not let us return.

The Master of the ship said, like a magistrate, *Sorry, Mistress Billington, but there is not the food to feed you on a journey back to England.*

And when our seven years were complete what did my husband get? What did we get for caring for all those weak, dying creatures, for surviving when most of them did not? The smallest plot in all the colony, that is what we got.

So when those hypocrites looked their cherubic faces my way and claimed themselves to be the saints and I, a stranger to God? Ho, ho, I said to them. They were as flimsy in mind and spirit as saplings. I feared them not, and loved their surprise at my bawdy self. With pleasure, my dears, with pleasure.

Call me a groundling, but I dare you to call me a thief, a liar, or a whore. Sure, those puritans did not say it to my face, but they knew what they were and so did I. And God. I liked to remind them of that when they passed by me and glanced out of the corner of their eyes, or when they stared at my good right hand, with dirt in the nails, that had been in God's clean earth, doing the gardening, planting seeds, presently reaching for our shared bread in the basket, or a sliver of butter.

When I saw Susanna hold her gaze at me, and Alice try not to, oh what fun, oh what joy it was to say, *God is always watching, isn't He?*

I preferred my breath to be nice and garlicked, keeping away the illnesses those dour ones kept giving us. The illness that killed my son John.

My sons, I did let them run. I did not keep them behind a fence. My boys could not even pretend to be a fox without those dour ones having their say in my child-rearing, tipping off the boy's fox ears and saying, *If you disguise yourself, you betray God.*

John the younger, rest him, came back after exploring for two weeks, wearing a string of shell beads around his neck, running to me, not scared, but asking instead if he could go back, begging me, really, to return with the Nausets. Of course I hit him, slapped the back of his head, sent him staggering forward, but I smiled, too. My boy was not afraid. The only things I hoped he feared were me and his father. When he died, how did *our* governor comfort us? By denying us his parcel of land.

I did not want Francis to fear these gnats, or take the same fate, so I encouraged him to leave as soon as he could. Even when the hypocrites drank—which they did, often—they tried to hide any enjoyment they got from it. The most fearful people I ever set eyes upon. Excepting my grandmother about her priest, my grandfather with the magistrate, and my husband about all snakes.

Which meant they could be easily batted around by fearmongers. Captain Myles Standish—Captain Shrimp, to us—enjoyed it. That hired soldier thought himself right and how easy it was for him to say to Bradford, *But the Savages, Governor.* Who was the governor of New Plymouth? If ye asked me, I would say Captain Shrimp.

John Billington

W orking in the field, cutting grain, John swung the scythe with more and more force. He stopped, looked out to the neighboring field. It should have been his son's land. It was owed to him. And today, he would purchase it.

When the colony's land had last been divided, each free man, woman, and child was entitled to one acre. His eldest son, John, was living with and working for Richard Warren's family, as was common to do, to learn a trade and ease the burden. When the announcement was made of who would get what parcels of land, Master Billington went to the meeting hall with the rest, not hopeful for the most favored land, for he was not well-regarded by those making the decisions, but he anticipated four acres. After all, he had two children and a wife.

Myles Standish read the names, the acreage, and pointed on a map of the locations.

Midway through the list, his name was called. *For Master Billington, three parcels*, Standish said, and pointed to a place near the brook.

They had given him three parcels, not the four he was due.

John Billington did not make the snort he wished to, nor the cry of outrage that, as a younger man, he would have made. Instead, he was patient for Bradford's ear.

Once the announcements were over, he followed Bradford through the crowd.

He waited until Bradford was exiting the group before he said, *Four acres is due me, Governor Bradford.*

Governor Bradford turned, but only halfway.

You were granted three parcels: one for you, your wife, and your youngest son.

The fourth?

Your eldest is not living with you, Master Billington. The requirement is that all members of your household must be living in your house.

Bradford knew it was common practice to send your eldest out to another family so that they could learn, not become too soft and reliant on their mothers, and also bring in more money for the family. No one ever spoke of living at home as a requirement.

Where does it say that, Governor?

There were no laws then, nothing written, anyway.

Every new situation calls for considerations.

These *considerations* were meant only for certain people. Bradford was walking away, toward his house, smiling at people around Billington's head as they passed, greeting, doing every trick to say to Billington, *You are not worthy of this conversation with me.*

John Billington was so angry he took to the fields, where he found himself on his knees. He had cried only a few times: When his wife agreed to marry him. At the sight of his mother in the stocks, her face painted over in white cream to hide the red, cracking sores. No one should treat a woman that way, even if accused a whore. She did what she had to, and for meeting the wishes of wealthy men, she was hanged. How little his people were given, would ever be given.

He worked the scythe, chopped the barley with more force.

Ever since he was not granted the land owed him, Billington worked quietly. He kept away from the hypocrites, did not go to Sunday service despite how forced upon them it was, unofficially. He developed a plan.

He went to Merrymount, thirty miles north, to seek out friends who understood, friends to dance and sing with, friends to help him forget. And when he was done forgetting, he took to fighting again. He wrote an angry letter to the investors but as soon as the letter was out of his hands and on the ship heading eastward, Billington had regret. It would not work, going above the hypocrites by writing to their lenders. Investors had no reason to believe him, a Billington. Truth has no value when riches are involved. One is loyal to the class closest to his own. The investors had yet to reply.

Finally, he conceded, if he wanted the land, he would have to pay for it. No one in the colony was to trade with Indians without approval from the puritan leaders and no one like Billington would ever be approved for trading. For the wealthy, a crime is rarely a crime. Living amongst hypocritical leaders required clandestine means.

Who traded with the Indians? Those who did the approving: William Bradford, Myles Standish, Edward Winslow. The colony leaders traded as it suited them, and their pockets were heavy with the profit he, John Billington, was forbidden from having. When Billington had extra gunpowder, extra ale—he got nothing.

Billington went to his friend Thomas Morton of Merrymount, who found a buyer for his extra goods. Morton was a lawyer from England, but one of the few good ones, who had, before coming to New England, advocated for his poorer countrymen.

Billington had met Morton when an invitation spread about a May Day celebration in Merrymount. Merrymount, built as a trading post, was loosely under Plymouth's jurisdiction at the time. When Billington heard the Plymouth elders rail against Merrymount for the community's Bacchanalian ways—men and women lying openly together, dancing around the Maypole, Indian and English trading and imbibing ale as suited them—John Billington knew he must attend. Anything the hypocrites despised, Billington had learned from the years living amongst them, was likely something he would enjoy.

Thomas Morton called himself not the leader but the steward of Merrymount. He was wary of the corruption leadership caused. On John Billington's first trip to Merrymount he saw how jolly the place was, which further put into relief the dourness of Plymouth. But Plymouth was where he had land, and where his son was buried, and he would not let that wretched lot of hypocrites run him out of town, too.

The spring before, Thomas Morton had been chased out of Merrymount by Standish's militia, as all good, profiting, dissenting men were. Chased away because unlike the hypocrites, he made friends with the Indians. He had fun and, most crucially, he made money. The Indians preferred trading with him to trading with the puritans. The elders did not tolerate money being made that did not benefit them. Standish ordered the militia to burn Thomas Morton's house and claimed they did so because of Morton's erection of the Maypole. The puritan leaders sentenced Morton to a small island off the coast, *until an English ship can return you to London*, Bradford had said. But that was a lie. They sent him to that rocky, inhospitable land to starve.

You'll pay for this, Morton said, pointing a finger at Bradford, his last words before he was put into the shallop.

Morton had friends in high places. If anyone could make that threat, and keep it, it would be him.

On Billington's last trip to Merrymount, his Algonquian connection told him Morton was not dead, but back in London. He had been kept alive by Algonquian friends sailing out to that island with food.

This past season, after Morton's exile, Billington had fished instead of hunted, to save his gunpowder. And now, with the arrival of new colonists, and the new parceling of land to them, this was his opportunity to purchase the plot before new property lines were made. He just needed a little more money. Just one more trade.

Morton had told him who would purchase at the highest price.

In case something happens to me, Morton had said, in an uncharacteristically solemn moment. They drank ale around the fire and revelers danced in the distance.

Billington had wanted that land ever since it had been denied him. But then, in spring his eldest, John, had fallen ill at Warren's house, and what that land represented was now so much more.

At midday, John Billington would meet a man by the lake that his youngest son, Francis, had discovered. Billington Sea, it was called, for the first Englishman to find it, named it. Billington Sea, though called differently by the man he was meeting. Two miles west, just barely out of Plymouth, which was a risk.

Billington was working the scythe, thinking of this impending journey, this one last trade, when he saw a tall man, red-cheeked and young, approaching him. As the man got closer, he recognized him as a Johnson boy. Well-liked, that family was. This Johnson had a bushy beard and thick brown hair on his arms. His sleeves were rolled up and in his arms was his new daughter, Mary, born two months ago. Her mother, Billington knew, as the whole town did, had died in childbirth.

Something must be wrong. Billington set down his scythe and went toward him.

It's Mary. We pray over her but the fever persists.

Billington observed the infant. She was splotchy from crying, but kept her eyes closed. He looked out on the field.

It was ye that convinced Lyford. And helped the Conners. Please. Anyone that could baptize.

Billington *had* persuaded the former Plymouth pastor, John Lyford, to preach to all of Plymouth, not just the puritans. They needed their children baptized, in the Anglican way, to protect them from death. The hypocrites forbade it.

When a boy was dying and needed an Anglican baptism, Pastor Lyford had agreed, though it took some persuasion. Sunday pie made by Eleanor and what trade items the Anglicans among them could spare. The boy survived. Lyford was found out by the elders and warned. Still, on Sunday mornings, Pastor Lyford led the puritan congregation at the meetinghouse and on Sunday evenings, at a commoner's house, Lyford whispered the Gospel to the Anglicans. Again he was found out and this time, Bradford held a big trial, the first in the colony. Lyford was accused of consorting with the *vile and profane colonists*, Captain Shrimp had the gall to say aloud. When confronted, Lyford burst into tears. He was given six months to leave the colony.

Since then, Plymouth was without a pastor, and one hypocrite elder, Master Brewster, served as lay minister for the puritans. Brewster would never perform an Anglican baptism. Would likely have Billington hanged for asking.

The infant whimpered, then fell silent.

Billington's corn looked strong, nearly ready to be harvested.

Let me see her, John Billington said, and outstretched his hands.

The young father put his daughter in Billington's arms.

She was lighter than he imagined and floppy. Billington had seen this look of a baby before. An infant on the *Mayflower*, two infants here, and his own younger brother. The infant, he felt certain, would die. If he went asking for a favor and found a lay minister to baptize the girl, he would be asking him to break the law. Billington would be risking his standing in the colony—not that his standing was much—as well as the lay minister's. He would also be risking their lives. A puritan pastor would be banished from the colony for such actions, as Lyford was, but the two commoners would be hanged.

Billington put his finger to hers. Slowly she wrapped her hand around his index finger. Her grip was faint. His sons never seemed this small. Never this weak. But he believed in miracles. A baptism had worked before.

Go to Master Tomlan. Tell him I sent you. He'll know what to do.

God bless ye, God bless ye, Billington, the young father said, nearly jumping.

If you want her to live, tell no one where you went or to whom you spoketh.

You have my word.

Johnson thanked him again and loped quickly through the field toward town.

Billington made his way home. One more trade and he would have enough money to purchase his son's acre. But first, he must ready his gun. He held the image of his dead son's face in his mind and vowed that he would fight for what was rightfully Billington land.

Newcomen

On the morning of the murder, John Newcomen arrived to the colony from Salem. He was not a puritan, though he suggested as much to get himself aboard the ship from London headed that way. He had landed in Salem and his plan was to then make his way south to Plymouth. But he had wavered after talking with the men at the boardinghouse.

A seaman there asked him where he was headed and when John Newcomen told him, the seaman repeated it like a question. *Plymouth?*

Another seaman leaned over the bar and asked, *You a puritan?*

Newcomen knew enough to say no, but privately he was considering becoming one. A literal interpretation of the Bible seemed better than none at all, as he had known as a child.

A fur trapper—telltale knife at his waist and fox head atop his own—and another man with high ruffles—likely a bank representative checking on a loan—raised their eyebrows.

The banker said, *Things are different down there.*

John Newcomen had done what he needed to do to get himself out of England. His stepfather was not religious, nor was his mother, though both obeyed the law by attending church. On weekends, his stepfather sent him to the village center while he drank his morning ale. Young John Newcomen was to sell his stepfather's ragged chickens, which no one wished to buy, and when he would come home with more chickens than sterling, his stepfather punched him in the face.

I'll do better next time, Father, John would say, spitting blood.

Very young he learned that to survive, he had to say something quite the opposite of what he felt. He moved into a boardinghouse as fast as he could, with a narrow bed he shared with another man, and ate as little as was necessary to keep his body moving. He'd saved his wages until he could buy this land.

Plymouth was the least expensive acreage he could find. The pamphlets advertised the most fertile soil and the investor he had purchased from, Thomas Weston, confirmed it. John Newcomen wanted a future, the kind a new place like this could give him. He chose a colony with seven years of experience. Newcomen had researched as much as he could from two thousand miles away.

He was not a lascivious man, nor a dancer, and he did not mind being around those who strongly believed in God. What harm could it do to believe?

They aren't your ordinary puritans, said the banker.

Nay, said the trapper.

The men laughed.

Who could John Newcomen trust in this new land? He did not know. He'd see for himself just how Plymouth was.

He thanked the gentlemen for the shared meal and retired upstairs that first night on the other side of the Atlantic Ocean. But he slept little, thinking instead of what the men had cautioned him against. When he had fatigued those worries, he considered instead every worry and wrongdoing he had done, or had been done to him. The curse of exhaustion was dread.

The next day, Newcomen arrived in Plymouth on a borrowed horse. It was late morning. The town was quiet, except for the lovely, tinkling sound of hammer against thatching pins, men high up on roofs. A hopeful sound. Men intending to stay a while and keep up what they built.

A woman walked toward him, introduced herself as the governor's wife, took from her basket a loaf of bread and offered it to him. He thanked her, felt a blush creep up his neck, and adjusted his collar. She said a pint awaited him in the meetinghouse and pointed the way. At first bite of bread, John Newcomen knew this to be the tastiest bread he had ever had. He called to her and said so. She kept her head down but returned the smile. John Newcomen thought he could not have asked for a better welcome.

Captain Myles Standish met him at the meetinghouse and marked on a map in the dirt where his land was. John noted with promise how near the brook he would be. Was this a preferred spot, he wondered, or did it flood? He did not know if he should be happy or disappointed—somehow the betwixt of these seemed impossible.

A bell chimed, announcing a meal, but John Newcomen had salted beef, the governor's wife's bread, and anticipation to power him all afternoon. He wanted to eat, but he wanted to see his land even more.

Eugenia would like it here. John thought of his fiancée, all that she might be fond of when she joined him, how welcoming it would look from her eyes, too, as he took himself down the trail to his land.

Alice Bradford

This place was once called Patuxet but renamed by Captain John Smith a more proper, English name: Plymouth. Ten years ago my husband led forty from the Leiden congregation, plus thirty-nine freemen who were not of our faith, eighteen indentured servants, and five hired hands to this coastal land. When they arrived in November, winter had gotten here first. Atop this hill were graves. Many Indians were dead from plague, as if God had cleared the land for us. As if God said directly to us: *Bring forth fruit, and multiply, and fill the earth, and subdue it, and rule over the fish of the sea, and over the fowl of the heaven, and over every beast that moveth upon the earth.*

The soil, we would quickly learn, was not rich, but there was a footpath to a small brook and other paths leading north. It would do.

We soon saw this was not unpopulated territory. This was Wampanoag homeland; these were their footpaths and their animal traps. William caught his leg in a trap, was flung upward in a tree, and had to be cut down. It gave the expedition quite a scare. Trails led through the forest in all directions, toward fields and ponds, toward neighboring communities. In the distance were their wetus, houses made from bent saplings. The Wampanoag had not ceased this place, but instead moved inland for the winter.

By August of the year of our Lord sixteen hundred and thirty, we had a longstanding agreement of peace with the Wampanoag leader, whom we called Massasoit, more than three dozen houses, and more than three hundred English residents. We had a meetinghouse and fort, a palisade to prevent attack, outdoor ovens, acres of nearly ripe corn, beans, and squash. But the number of English coming to our colony was decreasing. Even our friends were acquiring land elsewhere, building homes along the coast. What agreements these men did or did not make with the Wampanoag, I cannot speak of. Captain Myles Standish broke soil in Duxbury. He said he favored the country.

The land here was stonier than New Amsterdam and the port was shallower than Boston. My husband had chosen an unenviable place, far less fertile than what was around it. Once he learned that, he wrote the investors and told them thus.

Perhaps we should move the colony, he said.

But I did not wish to move. These buildings, these houses, these fences, all that work so that we could harvest a few more beans? This was my home now.

Thankfully, my husband's complaint was not persuasive. The investors told him, *As long as you have bread and fish.* They told him it was far better to be in an unenviable location, because there would be less threat of an attack. So here we stayed.

But when people complained—*The land is wretched, I shan't move my plow across it on account of all these stones*—William was the first to defend this land and, instead, find wretchedness in the people for their want of easy labor. We needed anyone who would choose to be amongst us, but this created problems, allowing in the ungodly.

On the last ship's departure, we sent back our largest bounty. We sent beaver pelts, worth more than the finest lace, to be worn around the wealthiest necks in London. We sent sassafras, sold to heal ailments, selling in London for two shillings a pound. We sent cedar, oak, walnut, and pine, chopped down to pay our debts. A cemetery of tree stumps, the northern land was now, burned to make way for more crops. We sent back two hundred pounds' worth of goods—what we owed our debtors annually—if not more, and waited for good news.

Two months later, Thomas Weston wrote to my husband with regrets. Our ship had been taken by pirates while nearing the coast of England, he said. So close we were to paying off a significant amount of our debt. In my less godly moments, I wondered if Weston was lying, if he had pocketed the profit, or made a deal with the pirates.

I would know which man on this ship out at sea was our investors' representative by how he exited. The one with the stretched-forth neck, who blinked his eyes, assessing the trees and fields for profit, that would be him. How he looked at my husband would tell me the state of our affairs more than what my husband reported.

We are doing fine, William often said. He would need to convince whoever this man was that we were a fertile, flourishing colony, not one in which colonists were departing and moving outward into Duxbury. It would only be time, I feared, before Plymouth resembled little of what we, with God's good grace, had intended for it.

On the incoming ship were adventurers—those betting on a future here instead of the weary one they left behind in England—who would be, initially, a burden to us and our storehouses. There were two wives to be reunited with their husbands, four Leiden friends who could not make the last two immigrations, and two children to be rejoined with their parents. More pressing on my thoughts, though, was this: On the ship was John, my husband's only son from his first marriage. I had not seen him for seven years. His mother, Dorothy, was my dearest consort. By dinnertime, I would be his stepmother. By dinnertime, I would be the stepmother to the son of the closest friend I ever had, and the closest friend I lost.

John's nearing presence brought me back to Dorothy. If he asked of her what would I say? And if he did not ask it would be worse. I worried he would see her in this house—the bed, the bowls, the baskets—and not take to me. In fables, a stepmother is seldom good. They send their stepchildren to eat the leaves even the deer cannot reach. They keep their stepchildren among the cinders. I was not on the *Mayflower* when they docked in New Plymouth, so he could not blame me for Dorothy's death. But had I not betrayed her? Had I not turned back?

DorAlice, the girls called us in Holland, led by Susanna, combining our names together as if it was the cleverest thing. We were the girls always dreaming side by side under the apple tree in Leiden.

Too close, I overheard Dorothy's mother say to mine when we were seven, as if there could be anything wrong with friendship.

Dorothy lacked vanity, a kind of luxury afforded the beautiful, not to have to work to look effortlessly fair. I was sturdy and dark, but my eyes were the color of new leaves. I had some pride about their color and therefore dyed my petticoat with larch to accentuate them. It took a while to grow appreciation for the plain, able body God granted me, but eventually, I did.

In Plymouth, I missed the confessions of the childhood friendship I had in Leiden. Dorothy knew all of my secrets and proclivities, before I knew how to restrain myself.

Perhaps all along was this latent feeling, considering what happened to her, my guilt at leaving her on the dock in England, after I had promised she would not make the voyage across the Atlantic alone.

Leaving Holland in the year of our Lord sixteen hundred and twenty for an English colony seemed then a sensible answer to the problems of being among the Dutch. Dorothy was not so sure. In Holland we could practice our religion as we wished, but there were other threats. The Spanish-Dutch truce nearly over. The children intermarrying, becoming too Dutch, losing their English manners. Or as William said, *Getting the reins off their necks and departing from their parents.* We sought a place untouched by corruption. Perhaps only in heaven does that exist.

My husband and her husband led the charge. I told Dorothy we would do this together. Guinea was considered first, but the year-round summer of Guinea did not suit our English bodies. I told her we would make a new community in the Virginia Colony, one in God's favor. I told her we would do this together, and then, at the last port before opening to the vast Atlantic, I turned back.

Once, William had said, about something the investors promised, *All promises are but wind.* Mine was, too.

After Dorothy's death, William wrote to me. He did not say how her death came to be, only that she perished. *I suppose the emptiness will pass with time,* he said. He wrote to me, I thought, because I loved her as much as he did. I would understand. But there was more.

Once, in my kitchen in Holland, before I had any children, William's arm brushed mine. The peculiar feeling when we were the only two in conversation.

I wrote a response full of the feeling of our shared memories of Dorothy and of my fondness and sense of loss for my late husband. Our grief brought us closer. A life with two boys, without a husband, was difficult. I was hopeful his letters might mean more than what they said.

In his next letter, William asked me to join him in New Plymouth as his wife. I was at my parents' table when I read it. He did not assume a yes, but in it were instructions. Sensing I had read something urgent, my mother came in, asked, *What is it?*

I read it to her.

If you deem me worthy, the ship is the Anne *and she leaves on the fifth of May. We can send for Constant and Thomas after.*

Thinking of my sons without me seemed far worse than what risks they would suffer in making the journey. He had urged Dorothy to leave their three-year-old son, John, behind, and I had consoled her by saying it would not be long. I was wrong. It took seven years and my urging to get her John here. By then, Dorothy was dead. I did not want to leave my sons behind.

At my hesitation my mother said, *You will say yes, of course?*

A wife does not make demands, at least not in the beginning, before she is even a wife.

I wrote back, *Yes.*

I left my two sons with my mother and tried not to think that I was sailing in Dorothy's footsteps, to be befallen as she had been.

Compared to what Dorothy experienced—the *Mayflower* nearly cracked in two in the middle of the Atlantic—my journey was pleasant. This was a ship now practiced in the transatlantic crossing. On my ship, the *Anne*, there were no stops along the way, no large storms that made the seamen draw the sails in. Lying in my bed at night, I imagined William's hands, how they would feel on my body. To be held again. His plentiful lips, how they would caress.

I first saw the shore of Plymouth in July in the year of our Lord sixteen hundred and twenty-one. A seaman called *Land ho!* one morning. I pinned my hair. I wiped my face with a few drops of beer.

Before sundown I was stepping foot on the shore, my sea legs wobbly, but a feeling I enjoyed, still rocking where I knew the ground was solid. I saw Susanna before I saw William. She had her beaver hat in the air, waving it at me, and I liked her immediately, all over again, despite myself. In Holland she was the girl who had teased Dorothy and me—perhaps, I see now, for how we kept our secrets. But here she would, I hoped, be my friend.

There was a gathering of friends to greet us, kind faces I had not seen in at least three years. Elizabeth and Susanna, waist-high children circling around, mothers calling for their sons and daughters to stay away from the water, baskets in the women's arms, ready to feed us. The men and women had a gleam—their labors in Plymouth were similar to those in Holland, but the walk to fresh water suited them, as did the air, and there was not the dread of a butcher to pay. The only work bell that rang was the one inside their hearts. Heifers had arrived and butter was churned weekly. The colonists' gauntness had recovered.

There were a dozen or more houses, with drifts of smoke coming from the chimneys. The air smelled of salt and cedar.

My eyes moved from person to person until I saw him. William. The two years not stooping over a loom for twelve hours a day, six days a week, had lengthened him. He was the tallest Englishman, but, as I later learned, all the Wampanoag adults were taller.

He stood upright toward the sun and took my hands in his.

Alice, he said, and embraced me.

The colony was watching.

I could desire him now, and in some ways this was the most desirous of all—acknowledging what had always been present, beneath all those years of acting how I should outwardly behave.

William, I said, and gave him a small kiss on his cheek.

His appearance showed the best parts of age. No longer youth's folly on his shoulders. He had made his mistakes. When Dorothy married him he was a man of promise, but an orphan, and five years into their marriage he was a man with two failed investments. He brought her to an unwelcoming land on a coast thick with threats—rumors of

Savages and wild beasts—and no friends or family to comfort, save himself. Without her son and without the daughter she buried three winters before. Without shelter. But when I married William he was governor of a new colony. Plymouth was repaying its debt at a rate faster than expected. Dorothy had a man betting on his future. I had a man at the height of his success. It was hardly fair that my fate should differ from hers, when I knew it to be that she gave more outward signs, every day, of her inward grace.

When I set foot on this coast, William was a different man, and I'd like to think that I was a different woman. My husband dead, and Dorothy, too. We knew what we could lose. Perhaps because of this, we cared more, now, for what we had.

We married the fourteenth of August, one month after my arrival, because a wedding takes time—a dress to sew, a celebration to plan—and our betrothal was also an opportunity to invite the Wampanoag and further build our alliance. Massasoit brought several men and a woman we thought of as queen. We saluted them with the shooting off of many muskets. And so all the bows and arrows were brought into my husband's house. Though dancing was against our faith, I admired the way they moved their healthy bodies. We believed the outward body displayed the truth of the inward heart. The Wampanoag were tall and lean, with thick black hair down past their shoulders, braided or pulled back at their nape.

It was a warm day. They did not wear as much clothing as I was accustomed and I knew not where to lay my eyes. Many had kind expressions. Though they did not believe in God as He would wish, they did conceive of many divine powers. They were men and women like ourselves. In this way, I saw they were not Savages.

The great sachem brought us three bucks. In England it was against the law to hunt deer, as only the King's men could do that. But it was as if we were at the head of the King's table now. We ate deer for days. It was a time of great cheer; everyone said so.

I did not consider it then, but above us, on a pole at the top of the meetinghouse, was the head of sachem Wituwamat, a Massachussett, on a stake. His black hair blew back in the breeze, his face half eaten by magpies, telling all nearby that we were a fierce colony. The uncouth John Billington asked Massasoit if he knew him, that head on the pole. Massasoit nodded. It was the only solemn moment of the day.

That first night we slept as husband and wife, Dorothy was in the room with us. Her bowls on the shelves, her blanket at my feet, her husband in the featherbed that was now mine.

I had not anticipated how marrying him would bring me too close to her. When he lay me on the bed, the pillows did not smell of her, for which I was grateful. But all she had touched was there, though arranged as William thought it right. When William was not home, I ran my hand along the coverlet, I touched the lips of the cups with the tips of my fingers.

Ten months after our wedding, William the younger was born.

Eleanor Billington

Knocking on my door while I'm trying my morning nap, who could it be but that no-good Captain Shrimp. I peeked through the window and told my husband to make himself scarce. I did not trust John to control his temper. He climbed into bed, put his finger to his lips, smiled, and became two lumpy pillows beneath the covers.

I opened the door to that Shrimp.

What will you blame us for now? I asked him.

This evening, he stumbled, *as I'm sure you've heard, we are having a dinner for the new arrivals.*

I made to sit down because I knew this would be good. Going to take him a while to clear his throat with these pleasantries before getting to what he was really after, which was for us Billingtons to keep our mouths tight when the newcomers arrived. Ha. We shan't. But I didn't mind listening to him request that we did.

But you see there is not enough room at the meetinghouse for everyone. And seeing how your husband prefers not to join us at services, and you've yet to contribute from your garden—

He stopped there, looked around the room.

What are you looking for, Standish? thought I, and I'd have said it, too, but I'd rather amuse myself with his ridiculous bug eyes making themselves so ungentlemanly. He was thinking I was going to fill in the space for him, that's why he'd stopped talking, or offer some ale from my personal cask, which I would not. I'm no fool. I shan't say for a man what he must say for himself. A disgrace.

Your husband has spoken against my good treatment of him, as you know. The governor would appreciate you give us this blessing and dine at home this evening.

He'd said it, so now he could look at me, which he doth with a put-on apologetic face.

I stood.

You've practiced this list, eh? Keeping tally. Perhaps I moved my arms about. *Well so are we.*

Mistress Billington, your allotment is just as equal as everyone else's. I've told your husband thus. You received just as many cows, just as many goats.

He was lying, he knew it. I just kept on my trail, I did.

Weston will see that, he said.

Oh, Weston coming. Now that *was* news.

So I, Eleanor Anne Billington, stepped forward more.

Trying to keep us away from the newcomers and Weston, are you? So we don't hurt your pocket by telling the newcomers the truth? Let the newcomers witness what you and Weston set us up for, sir. I hope they have wits enough to get back on that ship before it leaves.

We will not be silenced. Standish took a step back.

You tell Governor Bradford, if he wants a more contented colony, Master Standish, it would be advised of him to keep the colonists content.

I put on my proper voice for the occasion of insulting him, and enjoyed the little screwing up of his eyes when I said *Master Standish* instead of *Captain*, as he preferred.

Good day, sir, said I, and opened the door, pushing Standish out of my house.

It was a sight to see. I winked at the righteous ladies in the gardens pretending not to witness it.

Once the door was closed, and Standish out of view, my husband popped his head up from beneath the covers.

Weston's coming, eh?

What are you thinking, Good Husband?

We'd started calling one another Good Wife and Good Husband, like the puritans did, as a private joke. The hypocrites did not like us talking as they did. But we had kept it up.

Oh, nothing.

Those hypocrites. Had we had theatre, had we been permitted any enjoyable pastime to release us from them, maybe that day would have gone differently. But there was no theatre in Plymouth—the hypocrites hated the way Shakespeare and Johnson had depicted them, the she-puritan who so overflows with the Bible that she spills it upon every occasion. They claimed the theatre was the bathhouse for Satan. All we had for amusement was punishment. The tears, pleadings, and confessions of court, the hangings and the whippings. Instead of the theatre, there was the stocks.

John pulled his pocketknife out and used it to clean the dirt beneath his thumb. He flicked the dirt onto the floor and I didn't mind this time, not at all.

I looked at John and instead of buttoning my cloak to work in the garden, I undid it. I always liked the thick black curls at the back of his neck, liked to see the sweat glisten there. I smiled and approached him like a woman doth. He leaned back against the wall.

Other voices were out there, passing by our house, going about their day, forsaking a late-morning pleasure like this.

I loved John's long nose, cold against my stomach. He went betwixt my legs and when I was good and wet he slid inside of me.

Listen, there is nothing wrong with a woman speaking of what pleases her. Perhaps if the dour ones did so they'd smile more often.

I took his buttocks and pulled him toward me, tease that he was. He was gentler than lovers before. Maybe you think that comparison should give me shame? It dothn't.

I always reached my pleasure before him. It was easy with us, like pulling a well-baked pie from the oven. But had I known how that day would end, I would have gone slower.

Alice Bradford

The women and I were in the gardens when we saw Captain Standish walking down the path. He was a choleric man, as well as the shortest in the colony, a veteran of the Thirty Years' War, and, aside from Master Billington, the least even-tempered. He was for many years both footman and captain because he was our only hired soldier. By the time of the newcomers' arrival, though, he had formed a militia of colonists. And on that day, I would come to newly appreciate him.

Morning, he said to us.

We were pleasant. We waved. Three pious women doing our good work.

Before we left Holland, Captain Standish taught our men to shoot a musket and wield a sword. Now William slept with his musket betwixt us. We had been a peaceful colony and lived in truce with the Indians, aside from the one time a potential threat was rumored to be close,

and Standish preemptively killed six Massachussett men
and one boy, though another rumor claimed the only
threat given was instead an insult about Standish's height.
Standish's main job was to anticipate any violence and end
it, and he had once proudly ridden back into town with a
Massachussett leader's head on his lap. His demeanor was
to me, though, at that time, a comical vigilance. He
disliked how little he was seeing—no battle, no Indians
attacking our colony, no hundreds of arrows in flight, to
which he would have his musket and barrels of gunpowder
ready. He asked often for more supplies—more muskets,
more gunpowder—and William usually obliged. He had
two lookouts at the two highest points of the colony and
spent much of his days walking betwixt them.

Standish planned our community for how it could be
defended. It was on the downward slope of a hill,
stretching toward the sea. Our broad streets, eight hundred
feet long, were wide enough to haul a cannon out into the
middle of the road and shoot into the ocean. The meetinghouse was a large square building made of oak, with
six cannons atop the flat roof. Each cannon could shoot
five-pound balls of iron. Beneath the meetinghouse,
Standish kept the gunpowder and iron balls. Squanto, our
Wampanoag interpreter, had learned English when he was
stolen for slavery by Captain Thomas Hunt years before,
but, with great cleverness, had been able to wend his way
back home to Patuxet. He told the Indians we kept the
plague below the meetinghouse. My husband did not

mind the rumor. Standish had threatened the Wampanoag Indians in Namasket this way in the year of our Lord sixteen hundred and twenty one, when he told them he would put the plague under their beds if they did not obey his demands. A month later, nine sachems came to Plymouth to sign a treaty of loyalty to King James. Before we arrived, the plague had killed more than half of their people.

Next to the meetinghouse were our instruments of justice: stocks, a whipping post, and a cage. On top of the meetinghouse was the head of an Indian and next to that waved the bloody linen Standish carried his head into town on. The meetinghouse was where we ate together, prayed together, and, together, punished.

These days, instead of fighting Indians, Standish squabbled with those he deemed the black sheep of the colony. Mainly, John Billington, who was frequently seen coming from Standish's lookouts, again requesting, my husband told me, that his plot of land be extended past the marshlands, or that he was deserving of a third goat. His requests gave my husband ire, but not yet real threat.

We women waited until Standish was past us to peek above the fence and see just where he was headed. The sight of him often portended ill but he was a person it delighted us to speak of.

Standish was standing in front of the house of Master Billington, whom we had not yet seen out that morning though the sun was striving toward the middle of the sky. It was ten, I would have said, the time men who have worked on home building are climbing down from their ladders, wiping their sweaty foreheads on their sleeves, and having a pint.

In Plymouth, for the first six years, according to our bylaws, no matter how much or how little work a person did, they were entitled to the same amount of food and beer and wool as the rest of us. There were some exceptions and some added benefits, for the elders. The indentured did not vote on this law, nor did the accused and those deemed guilty of committing certain crimes. This was for their protection. Until the lands were separated, we all had to share the work but we divided the harvest equally, aside from what we grew in our private gardens. Many grumbled that the Billingtons, given the amount of time they did not spend in the fields, should get less than the rest of us, but still, my husband, in his benevolence, gave them equal share.

Captain Standish knocked on the Billingtons' door.

What's Billington done now? Elizabeth said.

I knew the reason, but I did not speak it.

Breathed, said Elizabeth.

Elizabeth had a calm about her. Her first son, Damaris, dead; her second, Oceanus, born aboard the *Mayflower*, dead; her Caleb, the age of my young William; her Deborah, four; a second Damaris, two years of age; and Ruth, a newborn. They were children who had been given acres to roam and a nearly worriless mother, who seemed somehow to view what she had from a knowing distance I myself could not ascend to. Or perhaps you lose so much you learn to no longer clench.

Eleanor Billington opened her door and Captain Standish stepped halfway inside. I'd have been more amused myself, had I not been privy to my husband's concerns—mainly, the economic risk of Billington sending blasphemous letters back to England. A new ship meant new people to be persuaded, new people to feed— prithee let them not be a burden—and new carriers of gossip to send Billington's disgruntled opinions back with them to London. Moreover, there was the representative, the direct line to our money. William would be keen to keep Billington's mouth as far away from him as possible.

It was not long before we saw Myles Standish reemerge and cross the threshold of John Billington's house, back- side first. His left leg caught on the threshold and he fell backward. Out of kindness, we averted our gazes. This was Myles Standish's lot, it seemed, to bluster and blunder. Myles Standish stood, brushed the dirt off his pants, and kept his eyes ahead. He walked swiftly past us women, this time looking forward only, and did not lift his hat.

Though the servants called him Shrimp, we women knew Captain Myles Standish as the Man Whom Even the Maidservant Would Not Marry.

Once, Myles Standish sent his newly freed indentured servant, Allard, to ask a maidservant's father if he could come to dinner that Saturday. A man inviting himself to dinner nearly always meant a proposal.

In hearing Captain Standish's request, the maidservant, Sara, asked of the courier, *And what of you, Master Allard?*

The courier understood this to be perhaps his only opportunity to save a woman he admired from an ill-suited marriage.

Would you marry me? Master Allard asked.

Sara said yes.

The courier returned to Captain Standish with great apology, but of course, not deeply sorry, as Master Allard married Sara two weeks later. Captain Standish outwardly supported the marriage, but he found small ways to punish his courier. When the time came to separate the parcels, for instance, he granted the courier marshland and the oldest cow.

In a colony as small as ours it was difficult to refashion yourself. Outwardly, he was Captain Myles Standish, but amongst us women, he was less. After that incident, he wrote to the sister of his first wife in Holland. Barbara joined us a few months later.

Every Sunday after Captain Standish married Barbara, we gathered in front of their house to begin the church processional. Standish beat a drum until the crowd gathered. He wore a long cloak and side arms, carried a small cane in his right hand and his musket on his left shoulder. In a line of three across, with the elders—William Brewster and my husband—by his side, they led the way to the meetinghouse for services. My husband always wore his long black robe and his musket, as did William Brewster, and the other men lined up behind them, each carrying their muskets as well. We women followed. Once inside the meetinghouse, each man propped his firearm beside him, furnished with at least six charges of powder and shot, as was custom, and which would later be law. Even on the Lord's day, the men were on guard.

It seems God is looking for a chuckle today, Susanna said.

She tipped her head to the two people coming down the path, toward Standish. It was the maidservant who had famously declined him. Sara was very pregnant and holding her new husband's hand.

Good day, we heard Standish say, in a harried voice.

It was an entirely ordinary day. None of us women saw the signs of what was to come.

Eleanor Billington

I'm punching the dough, right, readying for my turn at the oven and I get to thinking. Talking. John's at the table cleaning his musket, waiting on his lunch. Pushing the rod in and out. Our son Francis, good boy, out in the field. One son in the field working, one son behind our garden in a grave.

We have every right to that meal as they do, said I.

He said nothing.

Master Billington. Ye hear me?

He held the barrel up to the light. Blew. A puff of gunpowder on his moustache.

We don't need what they are giving. I'll walk on by that way, tip my hat, let Weston know I'm watching. Maybe hold my musket in my right hand. Scare him a bit.

John put on a growly bear of a face, but I knew he preferred to let the spiders find their way out of our house than smack them himself.

My sons, as I said, they liked to wander. Six months here, it was my youngest, Francis, that climbed the tallest tree at the top of the hill and spied with his great eyes a lake. He ran to tell Standish, sweet naive boy that he was, wanting to make the soldier proud of him. Standish called him a liar.

My son came home crying.

So I went to Standish.

I said, *How dare you call my boy a liar.*

Apologize, said I.

That scoundrel would not. I took my boy's hand and marched out of the meetinghouse and past it.

I told my boy, *Show me.*

I could not climb as high as he, but I could ride a horse faster than any other woman. We took our neighbor's horse—nay, *borrowed,* for I returned it—and rode two miles west.

Betwixt the trees, there it was. The smoothest, biggest lake I'd ever seen.

Francis Billington Sea, I said to him.

We whooped and called it across the water. There was no one to hear us, but the birds took flight. How proud I was of him.

We went back to Standish the next day. I told him I'd seen it with mine own eyes. I thought his eyes would fling from their sockets. Since my boy had found the lake, it had to be named Billington Sea.

I punched the dough harder. That Weston, that Standish, that Bradford. All of them disrespecting us so.

My husband made to leave with his gun.

Where you off to? I asked him.

An errand, he said.

An errand? I said. *Only errand you've ever done without saying so is going off to find more liquor.*

He snorted. I knew he was up to something, but whatever it was, it was his business, not mine.

Perhaps I should have called my son to follow him.

Newcomen

After lunch, John Newcomen walked past the palisade, past the guards, out again into the fields, out into his land. The palmy green leaves of sassafras in the undergrowth, swaying in the wind, the tall thin pines, the heavy-trunked oaks and maples letting in shaded light, the gentle sound of fresh water from the brook. If ever he had known God, he'd known Him in the forest. Now the bed of needles his feet stepped upon were his, as was everything his eyes and the trees would let him see. He stretched out his hands as if to hug it all, all ten acres.

He noted what trees would be best for lumber. He was ready to begin building.

Eugenia was waiting for him to send a letter and money to board a ship to bring herself to him. He wanted to work quickly.

As soon as the house is made, I'll send for you, he'd told her seven weeks ago.

They were at the shore he would depart from, over-looking the waves of the ocean. Sun close to setting, his last night in England.

She frowned.

He kissed the tip of her upturned nose and tried again. *Before the next harvest.*

Eugenia would not lay with him, despite every way he tried, even whence he proposed, even on his last night. She was waiting for the ceremony. He did not know a woman's body intimately and did she know it would make his want for her stronger? But what if he perished?

She was unmoved.

John Newcomen walked his property line and thought of her, wanting to know the edges of what was his, and absorb intimate knowledge of where he should set their house, where she would plant her herb garden, where their children would roam.

He found an oak tree, an ideal tree to begin his house with, and while he felled the tree and measured with his feet what he would need, he thought of her.

Here he was, in his future. The one he'd skipped dinner on Sundays for three years to afford. If his mother were alive she would have been proud of him. He'd done what they'd always wanted to do: He had escaped rotten England, and if she were still alive he would have sent for her next, after Eugenia. He looked at the rocky soil. *Our children will help clear these stones. We'll mark their height as notches on the walls I build.* When first he had watched

Eugenia betwixt the trees, with her younger siblings, hanging laundry and singing them a song, when first he saw her thus he thought, nay he knew, Eugenia would make a good mother. It pleased him to think of her living here, this land he could bring her to, this house, these fields, these birds, this brook, this future.

She was a fair woman. Someone who believed he could do what he promised. He was a man who needed someone to see in him the bravery and steadfastness he wanted to see in himself but at times did not believe he possessed.

Newcomen had made progress on the tree, nearly felled, but his revelry was interrupted.

Hello there, a man's voice said.

He had heard no man approach. John Newcomen turned around. The voice was confident, which somehow made it eerie. But it was only his new neighbor to the right, crossing their shared boundary. A bony man, with dark curly hair and a downward gaze.

Billington's the name, the man said and held out his hand.

Newcomen reminded himself of who he was—John Newcomen, a landowner, not a servant—and gave Billington a firm handshake.

It seems, Billington said, *Standish has told you what is mine, is yours.*

Newcomen looked around.

You are building on my property.

Newcomen stared at Billington, trying to assess from what was before him—moustache, worn clothes, greying tooth—how much power Billington had and, therefore, how he should respond.

Are you dumb? This is my tree you've cut into. And now you owe me for it.

I'm just following the map I was given.

I'm sure you don't want any trouble. Your land starts there, he said, and pointed to a tree three or more acres away, which would have reduced Newcomen's acreage considerably.

John Newcomen thought, *I've been out here all morning. Why are you waiting until now to tell me?* But also, *This man is lying.*

John Newcomen said, *Is that so?*

Billington nodded his head with exaggeration, as if Newcomen were empty-headed.

I'll inquire again with Standish.

I wouldn't trouble him, Billington said. *Best just to take my word. Over there, now, by the pine, not the oak. You can leave this tree.*

Newcomen looked at the oak. He looked toward the pine Billington was claiming was the start of his property line.

Tell you what, you leave it here, don't need to pay me. It is a waste, as I wanted the shade, but seeing as you are new and did not know . . .

On the ship over, John Newcomen had sworn that in his new home he would be a man who did not let anyone treat him like his stepfather had. He seemed to always find a man, or a man found him, who reduced him to the boy he once was.

If that was where my land began, Captain Standish would have said it. Nor am I your free labor.

His ears were hot.

Now, excuse me, Newcomen said, and turned back to chopping.

This would be his life here, next to this man? In front of Billington he would be composed, but inwardly he was shaken. His neighbor was slender but tall. Could Newcomen defend himself against him? He thought so and kept on chopping.

Billington made no motion for some time. Newcomen kept on with his work. He gathered thorny vines to use to pin in the two goats he would be given. One cannot let another man know, especially when first meeting, just how easily shaken he can be.

Newcomen finally heard his neighbor's boots moving away.

Billington turned. *You've been warned.*

Alice Bradford

After checking on the dough and finishing the mending, I could no longer put off my day's real task of warning Master Billington, by way of his wife, of what might happen if he repeated his ill behavior. Though I had lived five hundred yards from Mistress Billington for six years, I had not crossed the threshold of her home. I told Mercy to keep up her work finding stones in the garden and, with Joseph in my arms, crossed over to the Billingtons' house.

The charges against her husband were serious. But knowing the Billingtons, I suspected they did not think of it as such. Captain Standish had recently been there, and I regretted that I had to come upon her second.

I rapped softly on the door, revealing my timidity, which displeased me. I knocked again, louder.

The door opened. In front of me was a woman who had, clearly, just emerged from bed. I was not to say,

Sleeping in? in my most pleasant voice, because that was not the way of a godly woman, especially a governor's wife, but it was on my tongue.

Eleanor Billington looked at me from head to foot. Where her eyes caught I made my own judgments. My corset was cinched, but my dress did not yet fit again since Joseph. I was a tired woman, which made it harder to maintain a love for God's creations, particularly myself.

Come to see me, eh? she said.

I cleared my throat.

Yes, I said and adjusted Joseph in my arms.

Inwardly I admonished myself for not being the mistress the situation called for.

Your husband mad at my husband for speaking the truth? she said.

I was surprised she knew, but tried to stay on course.

That letter disparaging us will not help the colony, nor your husband.

As I spoke, Eleanor flicked something from her arm onto the floor. I hoped it was not a flea.

Her hair was not covered and the unruly strands— which is to say, nearly all of her hair—had freed themselves from the bun she must have made the night before.

I felt wretched in her gaze.

We have to get along, I said. *And that cannot be done with lies*, I thought, but speaking thus would have only provoked her.

I continued. *Prithee speak to him? Persuade him thus? The governor has taken pardon before. He is a benevolent man.*

Why was I putting on my pleading voice for her? She looked as if she would spit in my face.

Good day to you, mistress, she said. Was she really scooting the governor's wife out of the door thus, without offering tea?

She picked up the broom and began brushing dirt toward me and over the threshold.

The tip of my dress was already ringed in grey though I'd washed it the day before. I didn't need any more dirt. I had been respectful. In my right arm was Joseph, sweet and asleep, but my left arm was free.

She watched me look around. She stopped her sweeping and cocked her head.

On the table by the door was a basket of eggs.

You have made a second wife of yourself, haven't you, mistress? No one would even know your dearest consort married him first.

I picked up an egg. What was I doing?

I flung it to the floor. The cracking sound made a satisfying crunch.

She shrieked. I hadn't known she could shriek.

Lady!

The yellow oozed onto Mistress Billington's broom.

Joseph wailed.

Before she could say more, as if to run from what I'd done, to make that part of myself go away, I rushed from the threshold. I closed her gate, fast—I'd never felt my legs could carry me so fast, except they could, and did, later that evening.

In the gardens, I saw Susanna's and Elizabeth's white bonnets duck back down below the chamomile. They'd been watching, as I would have, too. I could hear Eleanor Billington. She had left her door ajar and laughed, a large laugh meant only for others to hear it. How could I let that lowly creature bother me so?

My husband was ahead, crossing the road betwixt our house and the meetinghouse.

He stopped and almost smiling asked, *Go well?*

I could see he had suspected that was how it would go. He wanted me to know firsthand how easy it was for a Billington to rile. I thought of Dorothy. I regretted I had not done it as well as she would have.

Other men were behind my husband, other elders, coming back from a meeting. There was the inevitable fight of what plots of land to assign, who would have new neighbors, the new arrivals to appease, the maps to finalize, the people to settle. And behind them, too, was John Newcomen. He'd bought acreage sight unseen while in England and, unfortunately for him, had been placed next to the Billingtons. John Newcomen going by was a cause for the women to stop and say hello. He reminded some of us of what our sons, the ones who had died as infants, might have become. I would say he was twenty. Eager and simple in manner, two reasons to look kindly upon him. I regretted that Standish had placed him so near the Billingtons. It was not a good or sustaining impression of what the colony hoped to be.

I offered John Newcomen a hello. He tipped his hat. I saw a blush mottle his neck. People gave deference so easily, I learned as a governor's wife. I was never pretty and never from great wealth, and as a girl, that was all girls had to give them deference, aside from piety. But here each new set of men tipped their hats and the women bowed because I was the governor's wife. If I was being honest, it was a new vanity of mine.

William gave his hand to me. Once the others were out of earshot, I whispered of the Billingtons, *Wretched lot, aren't they?*

My handsome William smiled, bowed his head, and guided us toward the house.

John Billington

John Billington, on his horse, nodded to the guards standing at the palisade, and rode through his field, on his way to meet the man he would trade with. But as he approached his field, he saw the newcomer had not heeded his earlier warning. An acre away, the man was, far too close, on Billington's own property, chopping down *his* oak tree still.

What's this? Billington called from afar, forgetting for a moment his vow with himself to begin with pleasantries. It was a recent vow he'd made after an unfortunate evening in the room beneath the meetinghouse, when a hypocrite had claimed he was inebriated. He was not, but that did not stop Captain Shrimp.

Newcomen, the man said, as if he, John Billington, had forgotten his name the first time.

This man was only a boy, the age his eldest son would have been. But this did not lend Billington any kind feelings toward him, rather it was an irksome reminder.

Newcomen's hand was outstretched, but Billington did not take it. John Billington folded his arms.

I told you, that's my land.

Newcomen apologized, said that Standish marked specifically this place, and the tree, as his. Newcomen said he was not to blame, that he was newly arrived, et cetera, et cetera.

Billington heard the name Standish and heard little else after that.

That man is set against me, doing this to provoke! Billington thought.

He saw yet again how Standish was intent to kick him out of the colony before he got what was due to him. Billington had been tracking his days and his land, suspicious the governor and elders were looking to take away what little they'd promised.

Here's what we'll do, Billington heard himself say. *That tree's mine, and we'll say your stake begins on the other side.*

He pointed just past the parcel he wished to purchase.

Newcomen seemed to think on it.

But it's not, Newcomen said. *Or rather, that's not what Captain Standish has told me.*

Billington smirked.

I don't want trouble, Newcomen said and went back to his chopping.

Billington took longer than he wished to regain his composure. When his breath was steady he told Newcomen to be careful and rode hotly onward to Billington Sea.

He met the young Wampanoag man at the eastern edge of the lake named after his son.

The two nodded.

The young man said, *Hello*.

He spoke in English, likely informed by two decades—his entire lifetime—of contact with English fishermen, trappers, seamen, and traders.

Billington brought out the powder and motioned for a show of payment.

But something gave Billington pause.

Billington was not sure how much English the young man would know, but he asked, anyway, *How will you use it?*

Was Billington's concern valid or was this the colony speaking, was this some English loyalty, the disastrous loyalty that never gives anything back, beat into the lower classes? Was this the fear, the wretched fear the hypocrites had so much of, leeching into him?

For defense, the young man said. The clear, obvious answer.

No matter, Billington told himself, when the beaver pelts were in his hands. Over went the powder, over went the pelts and wampum, and none would be the wiser.

The two men nodded, and each man turned back toward the way they came—Billington on horse, the other man on foot.

He'd done it. He'd saved enough to purchase the parcel adjacent to his property out in the fields. But that elation was short-lived. He was struck with fear. *What if they've already given it away?*

He finally had the means to pay for it. Of course it would disappear.

He had to go at once to Standish, or Bradford, and as kindly as he could muster—given their wretchedness—inquire about purchasing the land.

Alice Bradford

I picked up the rising loaves from the house and walked toward the outdoor ovens. Beneath the roof where my husband worked, William the younger held the ropes to two little goats. I left two slices of bread and meat folded in cloth at the base of a tree for both of them and told them not to work too long without eating. I tried not to dote too much on William the younger. My husband cautioned me that it would be the cause of his ruination.

Dorothy and William's son John had a grievous temperament, William had said. But I'd known him for four years. Perhaps he was just shy. I witnessed William's scolding of Dorothy for letting John hide under the table during celebrations and under his mother's arm during sermons, to which Dorothy always replied, *Yes, Good Husband*, but kept her son close, stroked her son's hair.

I wish to obey my husband, but my body says otherwise, she had confessed to me.

I told her I understood, but I did not. A child was a child, a thing to be molded by his parents. She was encouraging his reticence. I had never had a child such as he.

I hoped John's grandparents had been more fair in their teachings, pushing him out into the world. I hoped, for my sake, that John had changed.

My children were not thus, but from their births, my first husband, and then my second, disagreed with me about them. Where would they sleep? I preferred to keep them close, to feel the rise and fall of their chests. When William the younger could talk, I was content to let him play toy soldiers and horses after he finished his morning chores, while William said we must raise his mind above the sillier diversions of childhood.

He must be taught geography, astronomy, history, and Scripture to ward against every child's sinful nature, William said.

William the younger walked before his first year. All my boys were more apt to try something before they knew how to do it than observe from afar, like John was, like his mother, Dorothy, was, too. When William, at three, jumped into the ocean before he knew how to swim I soaked my clothes saving him and predicted, correctly, this would not be the last such occasion.

❧❧

At the ovens, Mistress Billington looked toward me, then quickly inserted her own loaves. There were half a dozen

84

loaves of bread and seven meat pies, lined up on the tables, cooling, and at least a dozen more to cook before dinner time.

No more room, she said.

Her voice so cheery to disrupt the day's work. I might have put my hands on my hips.

If we can't eat with ye's, I still must feed my family, she called.

Honestly, I said, and turned to go.

The ocean glistened in the sun. The ship was getting closer, but I had been wrong about how long it would take for them to arrive. They seemed to be stalling there, not moving toward us. Was something wrong?

What had Dorothy seen when first her eyes set upon this place? Arriving in November, with snow falling, three dead already, and half the people too weak to stand. With the Master of the *Mayflower* urging all hundred passengers out, out, in a hurry, so he could get back to England. While the snow melted on her eyelashes. With no shelter. While she drew her thin wool coat to her neck. Plymouth was a sandy beach and the terrifying unknown behind a thick forest.

The crew was sick by then. Scurvy ran through all of them. Old wounds, long thought healed, reemerged. Hers, too, I'm certain.

I imagined her huddled with the infirm, her teeth wobbly, her gums bleeding. Seven damp weeks on a ship designed for cargo, not people. She left Holland in June and thought she'd be here by mid-July. Instead, there were two delays and a change of ships. She arrived in winter. Months in the tween deck and six weeks of waiting for a house to be built had moved them all—or perhaps just her—toward a reckless mind.

❀

Once, in Leiden, when we were gathering the hens' eggs, the week after her daughter had been born, unbreathing, she told me she felt that suddenly she would die. She did not want to die, she said, and she lay down in the stiff yellow hay of the chicken coop. I listened to her and had on my sympathetic face, but as I did so I also wanted to yell, *Get up! Get up!*

Her elbows rested on a hay bale wet with hen dung. Her dress was turning yellow at the hem from muck.

I thought of all the rose-colored ways of speaking, how I could affirm to her what she did not believe about herself. That she would have another child one day, if God deemed it so. That William could have married anyone but choose her. *He had his choice of women in the congregation, but he chose you.*

Why is God punishing me? she asked me, and I thought about how beautiful she was. She shook her head, as if to shake away a second version of herself. *I didn't mean that. Don't answer my vanity thus.*

One cannot reason a person out of something they did not reason themselves into. I see that now. My father was a solemn man. But her tendency toward sadness benefited me as much as I was agitated by it. Her belief in me was tied to her disbelief of herself. It was not just her I missed. It was myself, who I was in her eyes. Except at the end.

Before William married her, she predicted he would marry me. I always thought her grander than myself, but never said it. I should have. I accepted the good light she shined on me, too, as I had with William, hoping it would or could be true. In doing so, though, I took too much of what she needed. Like a cat I purred, ignorant of how she gave me the belief she needed for herself.

It was easier as girls to worry together and perhaps easier for her to dream then, too. All that future out there, untried. In youth, nothing significant had been lost. I could still sweeten the smell of her future. She was not yet standing on a vacant shore with everyone around her dying.

Maybe we are made with these tendencies toward sadness. She took my leaving with grace. Perhaps I'm thinking too highly of myself, anyway, to think it mattered. Perhaps her acceptance of my betrayal was necessarily tied to her tendency toward gloom—she had expected all along I would leave her.

But that day in Leiden, with the chickens, she got up from the hay, and brushed off her elbows, and did her share of the chores.

※

At the nearby table, Susanna set her loaves down to cool. She leaned over them, inspecting, and frowned. She was as critical of herself as she was of others. Elizabeth sat darning a man's sock, preparing for the ill condition of the new colonists' clothes, as she wished there had been someone on the shore to do the same for her own family when she had arrived here.

The bread sizzled and cracked, one of my favorite sounds, as we women worked.

What say ye, an hour before we must feed them? I asked the women, though my intention was not to know the answer—which I knew myself. My intention was to remind the women the haste at which we needed to keep working.

Susanna nodded and pointed to the bloody linen waving high above the meetinghouse.

Nice welcoming sign, isn't it? Susanna said, more to Elizabeth than me, for it was a criticism of Captain Standish, perhaps, and by extension, my husband.

Four years ago, Susanna's husband had helped heal our Indian ally Massasoit from death with fruit preserves and chicken broth. Susanna's husband had scraped his tongue clean with his knife, and the man lived. After, Massasoit had told Susanna's husband that the Wessagusset sachem

Wituwamat did not like us. Twenty-five miles to the north, in Wessagusset, was a trading post settled by rowdy Englishmen, led by Thomas Weston's less-equipped brother, Samuel.

When Susanna's husband came back with the news of Wituwamat's dislike, Captain Standish said that we must counterattack to signal to our neighbors that we were not a meek, fearful group. Prior to this, my husband had worked to maintain distance from the settlers at Wessagusset, Englishmen who, when they first arrived in Plymouth, ate two months' worth of our meals from our storehouse, stole our unripe corn on their way out of town, went to Merrymount, and drank their money away. Some had become slaves to the Massachussett, so destitute they were, and sold the clothes off their backs for a peck of corn. It was not the way for Englishmen to be.

William agreed to Standish's request, I believe because of loyalty to his English brethren, however heathen they be, and to quell what confidence it might give the Massachussett. One evening Standish invited seven Massachussett men to Wessagusset under the pretense of trade. Pecksout, who Myles Standish had not met before, laughed at the sight of Standish.

You are no taller than a sapling, he said. *Are you a man?*

It could have been a joke, but Standish never took well to criticism, especially about his height.

Standish chuckled, but within minutes he locked the door behind them and gave the elders the cue. They stabbed the Indians with the knives around their own necks. One boy who would not cease to go away was hanged. But a boy hanged is not a thing to speak pridefully of so that part of the event was not much spoketh. Standish rode back on his horse into the colony at dusk, with the head of the eldest Massachussett, Wituwamat, wrapped in white linen. It was a joy to see Standish arriving home with the head of an Indian and not his own gone. He erected Wituwamat's head on a pike at the apex of our fort—a warning for all the tribes to see.

Standish took pride in his own might, and a week after the head was erected, the bloody white linen was erected alongside it. The rumor in the area then became that we in Plymouth were violent, unpredictable, and vindictive. This was the intention.

Let them think that, William said. *If it keeps us alive.*

My husband sent good news to Leiden, along with the invitation, yet again, for our pastor John Robinson to join us. In an earlier letter, Robinson had inquired about the Indians. Now my husband had good news: *By the good providence of God we killed seven of the chief of them.*

But Pastor Robinson, the man who knew I had been untrue in my confessions as a girl, but never stated so directly—just a lift of the eyebrow—sent his regrets. He was much too needed in Holland, he said. But he also sent his admonishments: *Oh how happy it would have been if you had instead converted some . . . where blood has once begun to be shed, it is seldom staunched for long time after . . . you will say they deserved it, but it is a thing more glorious in men's eyes than pleasing to God to be a terror to poor, barbarous people. Once there is bloodshed, there will be more.*

My husband did not expect such reproach.

How doth he? Judge me thus from halfway around the world, knowing not what we experience, said William.

This was, I know now, a premonition.

Pastor Robinson also warned of Standish.

Pecksout's taunt of Standish's stature was hardly cause for murder, Robinson said.

Standish's problem, according to Pastor Robinson, was pride and self-love. I did not disagree. Pastor Robinson cautioned William, saying Standish's temper was an outward sign of his ungodly heart.

But Captain Standish and my husband were not dissimilar. Quick to see threat and quick to act upon it. I did not doubt my husband was godly, though sometimes he seemed to have an excess of yellow bile. When a man betrayed him, he did not forget. When a man spoke ill of him—like the lusty seaman aboard the *Mayflower* who had bragged about hoping to throw half of the Leiden pilgrims overboard before landfall—William said that God would place a just hand upon him. The seaman was the first to fall ill and be thrown overboard, so God did what William predicted. But John Billington?

Well, God tests.

On my first twenty-fifth of December in Plymouth, instead of building the palisade, like the rest of the men, the strangers said it was against their conscience to work on the Lord's Day. By noon the strangers were out in the grass playing stoolball, drinking beer to excess, and laughing as we worked. By early afternoon, William stepped down from his ladder, marched over to them, and grabbed every bat he could reach.

He held them in the air, shook them, and yelled, *This is not the time for leisure!*

The strangers stopped their laughing and looked at him.

He flung the bats as far as he could. One landed near a bassinet and the baby screamed.

I'm sorry, but it is against my conscience that some should work while others play the devil's games. No more revelry or gaming as we work. If Christmas is so important to you, stay in your houses.

Master Billington said, *Master Bradford, we always celebrate Christmas this way. After all, this is an English colony.*

The crowd grumbled their agreement.

William stood very still and said, *That was England. This is Plymouth.*

❦

So you can see, there was the choleric about my husband. I hoped the arrival of the new colonists would not provoke him. Perhaps Pastor Robinson thought my husband's motivations were too base, for how he also behaved when instigated. Would my husband give in to the earthly wish for dominance? I wished to speak these thoughts to someone, but Dorothy was not here and it was my role to remain quiet.

Alice Bradford

In the afternoons, William often read Scripture. He liked to convene with God before taking his daily walk around the colony, then getting back to his labor.

Instead, on the day of the newcomers' arrival, I found him at his desk writing. A letter, it could have been, but I sensed something else. He stopped with haste at the sound of me kicking the dirt off my boots. He put the quill back as if he had done something wrong, or I had. That he had been immersed and inured to sound. He closed the pages of a book.

Good Husband, I asked. *What mischief are you inviting?*

He turned, but not with the kindness I knew him to have. Rather, with agitation.

'Tis nothing.

He got up and took his cup out to the front of the house, where I had set up the pails for washing. So many dishes to clean before the newcomers arrived and so many to wash a second time that evening whence they finished. They said fifty were coming, mostly from Leiden, but always the investors seemed to sneak a few in from London, and those few grew our profane lot. Some brought their own bowl and cup, but many owned not even that. I had learned to be prepared for the people who took more than their share of pie and did not offer to help with the dishes. Whatever my husband was writing, I suspected it was intended to uproot the problem colonists.

He came back in, said, *Mind me, Good Wife*, and dashed his eyes in the direction of his desk.

I'll be at the water, he said, and shut the door.

Joseph was hungry. I lifted the oiled cloth so I could watch the sky as I nursed. William was going toward the shore. I settled Mercy with a slice of bread and a bucket of blocks and went to the rocking chair. So close to the desk. The book William was writing in, I could see, was beneath pamphlets and maps. It was an untidy desk, whereas when it had been Dorothy's father's desk, its surface had gleamed and was nearly empty. More for decoration than use.

In the drawing room, we girls once pulled out the drawers when her father was at the market, or away, anyway, anywhere but near the house. Inside was snuff, letters with red wax seals, and a secret stash of tea. That combination of scents was stirring, and I hadn't thought to smell it again here in Plymouth. I leaned forward, my left arm cradling Joseph, my right arm long enough to reach the drawer. I pulled it open, inhaled. Still there, that smell, and I was back in the drawing room, back with Dorothy telling me about Johannes. The pink ribbon her mother braided her hair with was highlighting the natural flush of her cheeks, and I begged her to tell me more and more, though she promised it was only one kiss, only that once.

He was Dutch. He wanted to be a painter. She met him at the market. She told her father he was tutoring her in Latin. She liked to press her head against his chest, to sneak his smell in alleyways and shaded corners of the house.

As Dorothy spoke, she pinched some tea from her father's drawer for us to share.

She said her father would forbid the union. I asked why, naive as I was then about loyalties and lineage.

He's Dutch, she said, losing patience.

Girls! her father called. He was coming down the hall, closer.

Is my desire delusional or is it good? she whispered.

I told her I did not know.

Johannes was the man Dorothy would have married, I believe, had her parents not forbidden it.

At the doorway her father said, *William Bradford is coming to dinner.*

Run along, now, Alice, he said to me.

And to Dorothy: *Tell Mother to take in her finest dress.*

Dorothy had flints of gold in her eyes. It was as if a breeze had blown in through an open window and thrust her life into new relief.

Though older, I was the girl to run along and Dorothy was the woman.

At that time, what we knew of William was what was whispered at church. He was a new arrival from England and had traveled to Holland alone. He had full brown waves of hair and one of the most alluring conversion stories.

He had nearly died after both his parents and sister died, too, and in a fever state he had a vision: that God had higher plans for him. William fell ill for weeks, then months, and was punished with the pleasure of reading books in bed rather than work in the field. One day he awoke with energy as he had not had since his mother was alive. A voice whispered to him, *Scrooby*. He walked at once—a half day's journey—to Scrooby, where he came upon the village mailman, William Brewster. Mailman by day, and by night a secret pamphleteer against the King, which Brewster printed on his illegal printing press. He was the host of private, forbidden gatherings, where people studied the Bible in his home. *There is no uncorrupted Church of England*, the group argued. *We must leave.* Bradford's uncles heard of where he went in the evenings and more directly than they were wont to do, said, *Do not believe what those puritans say.* His uncles' persistence persuaded William further that he was following the right path.

If William had stayed with his uncles in England, he would have lived a comfortable English life from his inheritance. But with one pair of worn-out boots and a sturdy ploughman's gait, the young William fled his uncles' home and followed Brewster's group to Holland. He came to Holland with no money as we knew it but the promise of his parents' inheritance. Here he was then, in Amsterdam, now a man of twenty-two, inviting himself over to Dorothy's house.

Dorothy walked me to the back door, but we stood at the threshold.

He wants to marry you, I said.

Dorothy said, *A dinner is hardly a proposal.* But she smiled and touched her hair.

I was eager to hear the details, pressing her, a preference for imagining. Happy, in a melancholy way, to watch it unfold while looking from afar.

Her mother called her away. Her mother's voice was always shriller than it needed to be when she called Dorothy's name.

The next morning, while laundering, Dorothy told me what had happened.

Her mother took up the sleeves of her own second-best dress for Dorothy to wear for the occasion, and Dorothy felt as if she were her mother. At dinner, William was proper, as he always was before we knew him. She was stiff with all the things she thought but felt she could not say in front of her parents. All her words felt childish. Her mother smelled of sour milk, which she whiffed on the dress while leaning over to pass the peas. She was reluctant to choose a husband, to think of marriage, and the dress further strengthened her reluctance. This spun her, at dinner, inward. She would have an ungrateful daughter and twitter around the house in nervous anticipation for someone else's future. Her face would show that she had frowned more often than smiled. All of these things I tried to assure her were not true, but she increased the speed of her words.

That evening, after William left, Dorothy warmed her feet at the fire and stitched. She told me she thought of this new despair, growing out of childhood, and as if that weren't enough, her worry was interrupted by the sensation that she had peed herself. She had not taken off her mother's dress. She stood in a panic and slipped the dress down her body. The backside of the dress was red.

The marker of womanhood had arrived, but more foreboding than that, she had to tell her mother. She took the dress upstairs and dipped it in the washbasin. Ribbons of blood waved in the water. Despite her scrubbing, the blood could still be seen on the dress. She took it to her mother, held it up, and apologized.

Her mother embraced her. And in her mother's arms, in her tight hug, she lifted her daughter slightly off the ground, and said, *Congratulations.*

When her mother inquired about Master Bradford, as we called him then, Dorothy said little. Dorothy told me she felt certain her love was for Johannes.

But her parents found out. Her father came home early and saw a kiss. He shouted Johannes out of the house. Dorothy tried to explain.

He loves me. We shall marry.

Too young, her father said.

And when Dorothy still persisted, he said, *Too Dutch*.

She was fourteen then, the age when our cousins were planning their betrothals.

I can ride a horse well, I can keep house, I sew, I—

Her father shook his head. He was balding. Betwixt wisps of hair, where, if he were royalty, a crown might reside, was a shiny white skull. He was not royalty, but he was of wealth.

It did not matter what she said.

But, Father, Dorothy said, and her father waved her voice away with his hand.

Her mother was gentler about the subject. She waited until the two of them were outdoors laundering to say to Dorothy, *Tell me about him.*

What did we know then about love, about marriage? Nothing.

He gripped her in the drawing room, he gripped her in the alley. She would not know another gripping in this way, because it was her first, but she knew this was not the thing to say to her mother. Dorothy stumbled and said the things she thought her mother would like to hear. About what he could provide—but he could provide little—and when that was clearly a misstep, she spoke of his good deeds, the outer signs that he was chosen by God, part of the Elect.

But that was too much for her mother.

Honestly, Dorothy, her mother said, and took the clothes inside.

She conveyed all of this to me while we sipped her father's tea.

Am I too vain? she asked me. *Is my desire delusional?*

In her eyes was the shimmer of tears before they fall. I did not know what to say to her, but I knew whatever I did say, I should be steadfast. I took her hand.

Let it be as God intends, I said.

Dorothy nodded with a wobbly chin.

But no answer had to be given, for what God intended was illness.

The next morning, smallpox seized her. She lay in her mother's bed. I went to her.

I deserve this, she said. *It is my desire.*

The pink sores on her face emerged first as faint circles, then ballooned with fluid that tightened her skin. She stared at them in the hand mirror, willing them to pop. But her urge to squeeze them was dampened by the pain it would cause, and her mother's warning of the deeply embedded pocks that would mark her face forever—if she lived through it—and mar her chances at a suitable husband.

It is my passion, she said.

But when her mother asked her to say more, she said nothing.

God tests, her mother said.

The fever increased the rapidity of her thoughts. Delirium, and she thought she saw Johannes in the doorway and she thought he kissed her in the morning.

Was he here while I slept? she asked me.

I assured her he was not.

She said she saw a woman with long brown hair, in a black mourning dress, standing at the foot of her bed, watching.

I'll die, she said. *I'll die from my desires.*

But she did not die from them, at least not then. Dorothy repeated to me all the family members she knew who had died from smallpox—Henry, Mary, Uncle—and asked me to entertain her, which I felt I did poorly, by telling her what a fool one cousin made of herself in front of a suitor and relaying the new wet nurse's blunders.

Dorothy spoke of the number of pocks she once saw on the face of her sister Katherine, when she lay in her coffin. Dorothy had half. Queen Elizabeth was rumored to have survived an extreme case and so, too, I reasoned, could she.

One morning, Pastor Robinson paid her a visit. She lay on her bed and confessed to God and to Pastor Robinson, *I have been vain. I have been prideful.*

If only God would spare me, she said.

Her desires were natural, Pastor Robinson assured her, as well as a test from God. I could not see how she spoke to him so openly, but death had not appeared so close yet on my bosom. Like all good conversion stories, hers was a far better one than my own.

Color began to return to her face. She showed again an appetite.

Did it comfort her to observe her own desire growing fainter and to know that she was one of them now, of the brethren who had confessed and joined again with God? It did not comfort me, because I was too vain to confess, too ashamed to admit my shame.

Before, when we were bored listening to the sermons, we looked at the faces around the church and whispered, *What do you think she did to bring her closer to God? And what about him?*

She no longer wished to play this game with me. Alone, I imagined the actions and desires of their lust, greed, and envy. In the days before I thought I really needed God, this made the church mornings go by quickly, but not as fast, doing it alone.

But that was years ago, the love of a young person, in vanity, looking for a more beautiful reflection. When Dorothy was well again, she asked if I would help her find Johannes.

But you've renounced him, I said.

I must first say goodbye.

Together we looked for Johannes in shop windows, clothiers, and bookstores. We stalled coming home from the market. No one had yet taken an interest in me unless at my father's urging, and I was happy to be conspiratorial with her, searching for one boy in a town of thousands. Six weeks passed this way and when I asked about him, she finally shrugged and said, *I never loved him*. But I did not believe that to be true.

One Saturday, at the market, while reaching for an apple, someone took Dorothy's hand.

We turned.

Johannes said, *I'm going to*.

His eyes moved back and forth over hers. He had threatened it before, the military. He was searching her face for an expression. He was looking for her to tell him not to do it.

Let go of me, Johannes, Dorothy said.

Her mother was close by, pressing the pears for ripeness. She could look up at any moment. I was standing an arm's length from her, a presence that could judge, perhaps, after all the days she had said she did not care for him at all.

The light made his face even more golden. She told him that she had confessed and that her love now was for God.

This was Dorothy May, so composed. This was the Dorothy May I knew her to have become, never distempered in public. A good girl, as her mother had praised her to be.

Her mother turned. Dorothy pulled back. He went away. A week passed.

Then one day a blond head poked around an alleyway corner. Johannes appeared at Dorothy's back door with a new haircut. He knew the trouble his presence would cause if caught. There were bug bites on his arms and legs. He was in new boots and wool socks the color of his grey sheep.

I'm going this afternoon, he said.

He was in front of her, those full lips, those new boots. He had done it.

Dorothy bit her lip.

But the Spanish, she said.

Only a self-murderer, she told me afterward, *would enlist in the Dutch military when the truce was ending.*

He had wanted to be an artist, but instead he became a soldier.

Dorothy's mother called for her from the drawing room. Dorothy left him this way. She told me she had wanted him to persist. William would have. William would have said, *Dorothy. Look at this!* He would have fought hard for her. And by the end of the conversation she would have agreed to be betrothed despite her parents' concern. All that, though, came later. Dorothy never heard from Johannes again.

William Bradford waited. For Dorothy, he needed more than an orphan's promise. We never spoke of this— wealth was too embarrassing to discuss—but even at fourteen I knew where I stood. Her parents were amongst the wealthiest. Mine were not. William was a good Englishman, our parents said, but even that was not enough for a family of her parents' standing. William knew as much. When his inheritance sum arrived, he proposed. In her vow to God, and soon, to William, Dorothy and I no longer drank her father's tea in secret. As happens, we were no longer one another's dearest consorts.

John Billington

He found Standish at the meetinghouse conferring with the elders.

Billington went to the group—Winslow, Bradford, and Standish—with a pile of beaver pelts over his shoulder. They looked at him with surprise.

I belong here as much as you, Billington thought to himself.

He lowered his head down to Standish's height and addressed him. *May I speak with you?*

Go on, Standish said.

Privately.

Billington knew three men against one would not be in his favor. Where one could be sympathetic or negotiated with at least, the third would point out what the other two forgot.

Standish placed his eyes upon the pelts and raised his eyebrows.

Very well then, Standish said, and motioned toward the stairs.

Billington could have spoken to Bradford. This may have been a better move, but it was Bradford he had first been so quickly dismissed by.

Standish and Billington went upstairs to the loft. The two men sat on two upturned crates. All of this prolonged the anticipation and Billington's agitation. He shouldn't have needed to do this. He set down the pelts and gathered his hands, pinching the skin betwixt his thumb and forefinger.

Billington said, *I'd like to purchase the land adjacent to mine.*

He hated that he was uncomfortable, sweating, not steady in his voice.

Standish smirked.

With what funds?

Billington motioned to the pelts. He lifted his cloak and opened the purse of wampum and sterling.

I did not know you to be a skillful trapper. What crime did you commit to get this?

Billington scowled.

Of course you accuse me thus.

Standish said, *In any case, the land was given to a man who arrived this morning. John Newcomen.*

Billington had worked hard to find these funds and as he saw it, if he were a puritan, he would have been able to trade openly with the Indians anyway, so what he did to get this was not a crime.

Tell him it was a mistake, Billington said.

I can't do that, Master Billington. He's working the land as we speaketh.

Why not purchase—and at this, Standish spoke of a low land with rich soil, which he described as the most fertile, with the most potential. Lies.

I want the land next to mine, not some marsh that even the deer do not visit. I want the land my son was owed.

Funds obtained illegally are no good here. Did you trade with the Indians to get this?

Prove that is what I have done.

Standish smiled. He put out his hands, palms up.

The proof, Master Billington, is sitting before me.

And there again was Standish's smirk and then a laugh.

Trading with Indians is, as you know, a punishable offense. Thank you for confessing thus.

I did no such thing. This was true, he had not confessed. He liked the way saying this suggested he had not traded.

Billington, when we prove those pelts came from the Indians, which we will prove, you will be tried for committing a heinous crime against the colony.

Billington heaved the pelts back over his shoulder.

You, Shrimp, are a crime.

Standish stood. *If I were you, I would apologize.*

He shouldn't have said it, but he did, and he would not apologize. Billington would reach for Shrimp, he would, or Shrimp would spring at Billington and not be punished, and then Billington would no longer have the pelts, the wampum, the land, or his freedom. Instead, Billington rushed down the stairs and out of Shrimp's presence before the man—and his own desires—could catch him.

Alice Bradford

I loved and envied her. I did so as a sister does, and when
we cut our knees—one of our last times climbing over
rocks as unwed women—we touched our blood together.

Dorothy said, *Now we are sisters*.

William Bradford proposed to Dorothy in the fall of
her sixteenth year. I thought they were illuminated by
God's good light and when they married at the Amsterdam
courthouse in December, I was the witness. At the courthouse, she shivered. As men and women of God, it was
understood we were not to make a fuss of a marriage
ceremony's earthly trappings. William reminded Dorothy
of this when she reached for the most fragrant hyacinth
bouquet at the market to take with her to be married.
They were grown in a greenhouse, where the gardener
approximated spring before its time. Therefore, the
flowers were not of a modest sum. One was to be modest
in all things. William believed that, and we did, too, in

principle. But young girls have fancy, which feels like freedom, which maybe is freedom. The fancy fell away for both of us in marriage. Not because of our husbands, exactly, and not even, perhaps, because of marriage, but because of time. We got older.

Meanwhile, my parents arranged more invitations for me. Dinner included my lazy third cousin, who inherited land in England and new congregates with money but suspicious pasts. I enjoyed the meals my mother made for the occasions, but not the dinner conversation nor the looks my parents gave me afterward. My menses had not yet come and, not wanting to be left behind, I was urgent for it to arrive.

One day, Edward Southworth came to dinner. He had a moustache that extended over his top lip and was naturally slender. These two things, like his temperament, never changed. He was at the cusp of old age. His hair was salt and pepper, with two orange strands framing his face, thin and flattened, even in the thick, wet air of Holland, where it rained more often than it did not. But his hands were soft, not cracked and calloused, but well-treated hands, as if he were a person who was kind to himself and that which he touched. Of the men my parents planned for me, he held the most financial promise. It was said he had descended from royalty but gave up that ease to follow God's higher plan and join us in Holland. With age comes well-worn ways, and thankfully for me, his ways were gentle. This assessment was one of the few I made at fifteen that I was not later embarrassed by.

I was happy. Nine months into our marriage, Constant was born.

Dorothy wanted to be a mother, too, and here is where things went wrong. A few months, and her stomach was not warmer to the touch. A year, and still nothing, and the women of the congregation murmured. Was William not performing his husbandly duties?

The midwife gave her a tincture. She gave her a tea. She told her to put a tail feather in William's morning porridge. Dorothy did what she was told. Months later, her breasts grew tender. Then blood.

Finding her in the kitchen, kneading bread to hide her eyes, I offered: *This must be the way God intended.*

I saw immediately that it was the worst thing I could have said, but it was what I had been taught to think.

God gave her more blood.

Please, God, she said.

Begging God was never God's way. Upon seeing her at church on Sunday, she told me what happened, both the blood and how she asked God for what He had not yet granted her.

She looked down and said, *I should have told Him nothing.*

To ask for anything earthly was to bring God's wrath. I could have cautioned her but I did not.

When I labored, Dorothy was kind to stay by my side, to never mention her own desire for a child. Though I wanted to ask, to speak of her sadness, I did not know how.

But in spring, her stomach blossomed. Everyone predicted a girl by the way she carried her, how gentle the baby was inside of her, not kicking like my second was inside of me, not banging against her ribs. A quiet one, a thoughtful one, as a girl can be. The labor was fast, which rarely happens with a first. She was born into the midwife's arms, unbreathing.

What's wrong? Dorothy asked.

I could not speak it.

What is it? she asked again.

She looked betwixt her legs.

The midwife put the infant in her arms. Dorothy's face showed recognition, then turned resolute.

There, there, she whispered to the newborn, kissing her purple forehead, her tiny nail beds, wiping away the white vellum that babies arrive in.

I stood back and watched her love her daughter, but did not leave the room, because my presence would incite the others to run in, cheer, speak too soon.

Dorothy insisted on wringing out her own bloody sheets.

Please, let me, I said.

No, she said, and walked in the slow aching way of a new mother.

Her family in Amsterdam did not yet have a plot to bury in. William chose one in Leiden, the closest to their home on Stincksteeg. It was a warm spring day at her daughter's burial. I tried to hide my stomach—it seemed a personal affront to grow another child in her presence. There was a large meadow and a small grave. We covered her with tulips.

Afterward, Dorothy stayed indoors for longer than William deemed appropriate. Dorothy said she feared that her own moral errors had caused her child to be punished.

William said: *This must be the way God intended.*

But I did not believe this any longer.

I put her cold hands in mine and said, *No grief is deeper than this.*

But still, she stayed indoors. Her husband called a doctor, who prescribed a spoonful from a bottle twice a day. He prescribed resting. Then she could lie in bed freely. I worried about her, but my days were full of two young sons. If there were a doctor on the *Mayflower* Dorothy might have been prescribed something, when it was her son she longed for.

One morning William came to my house. He knocked on the back door. I heard it creak open. I was in the kitchen rolling dough. At the sight of him, I felt a flush. I hoped my cheeks were not red, that there was not a creeping rash rising from my chest and up my neck.

Body, I thought, *please do not betray me.*

We had not been alone since I bid him good night one evening after church, when I was fourteen and we had found ourselves the only two left lingering. We would not have been alone in the kitchen, but my husband had left for the silk mill early that morning. There was a debt to pay to the butcher along the way. Our two sons were, miraculously, working quietly together in the other room, preparing kindling.

Could you call on her, today? he asked me. *She's not well, I fear.*

I tried to think of what he was saying and not the way he glimmered—*His eyes? His smile? What was this?*

I was to come this afternoon, but I will come early and bring pottage.

He thanked me, smiled, turned, and as quickly as he'd come, he was back out the door and down the alley.

When I went to visit Dorothy, she said William had asked her to go to the New World. She had been crying. I had Thomas on my hip and Constant was running toward the fireplace. I grabbed Constant by the arm and tried to sustain my attention to Dorothy as best I could. She did not have children yet and though she was sympathetic, I worried my attention to my children—that change to our friendship—was to her a laceration.

Where? I asked.

He said Guiana, maybe, or the Virginia Colony.

Nothing then was settled. They considered Guiana and Florida, but Guiana was too hot for our English bodies and Florida was too close to the Spanish. The elders said they were men of the north and they would stay north.

Why does he want to leave?

He said the Spanish could attack Holland at any moment. He said our children are becoming too Dutch.

Now that the peace treaty was nearly over, many in Holland were fearing the Spanish. And the younger people were losing their English manners.

He says that. But it's money, too, Dorothy said.

Being a fustian weaver in Leiden was not going to give him his autonomy. He tried once to sell his textiles directly to merchants. But the Dutch government required all textiles to have official approval—a seal—and in so doing took a tax. And the tax was too steep for William to make a profit.

Therefore, his investment in the textile company failed.

William believed that to succeed as God intended, he had to go elsewhere. It could have seemed then as improbable as once thinking the world was round, to leave our community in Leiden to go halfway around the world.

Going where? Dorothy had asked him.

And when he said a colony in the New World, she asked, *With the Savages nearby? And you think the King who outlawed us will now give us a charter?*

William could convince. He believed his childhood vision was God's way of telling him to follow a more difficult but higher path.

Dorothy told William, finally, the reason that lacked all argument, the reason that was a feeling, that was the truth: She did not wish to be so far away from her daughter.

Plenty of women had lost children. Her aunt had died in childbirth. Every woman knew that preparing for labor was preparing for death, both their own and their child's. We planned our will and rehearsed our last testament.

Perhaps the losses are God's way of saying He has other plans for us, he said.

He said this gently, but Dorothy said, *No*. A final *No*, lacking emotion, a *No* that would not be persuaded.

Scripture could be used for any claim.

William, imbalanced in humors and out of argument said, *Our daughter is dead. That body in the grave is not her.*

This was more than Dorothy could bear, but she bore it.

In recalling the discussion with me, Dorothy stood and concluded, as if talking to herself, *I cannot be the wife who does not give him what he needs.*

She wiped away her tears.

She said he asked for so little, that she needed to give him this. I did not agree, exactly. It seemed to me, as was often with her, that she could not see how much he was asking for. To leave your family and your friends for what?

I readied myself to tell her I would not let her go alone.

I stood, because I knew I should get home and prepare dinner for my husband. But the conversation was in its careful place. As women, we rarely talked this way, so freely as we once did as girls.

Seeing Dorothy and knowing what it would be like without her, I said, *We'll do this together, you and I.* I should not have said this without my husband's approval. But I did. It was her I loved. We would live next to one another, in the old world or the new one.

I wondered if William was planning this, in part, for her, too, to help lift her from her grief. That perhaps she needed to leave that tiny body in the grave. If she was to go, I would go, too. But I had to persuade my husband, without it seeming as if I was persuading him. All afternoon I thought on it. When he came home from the mill that evening, he whistled through the front door. I was thankful he was in a boisterous mood.

Good Wife, he said. *I've been with William Bradford.*

God was granting me such good fortune. What blessing that God wished for us to be together.

And what did he say?

He wants to make a colony in God's likeness.

And you said?

I told him we will go.

But the plans to leave Holland faltered. No one wished to fund our journey to the New World, except the Dutch, who offered to take us to New Netherlands for free, but then we would still be living in a Dutch colony, only this time along the Hudson River. To do so would be to move ourselves halfway around the world to be again among their permissiveness. As William noted, nothing was free, and to be taken by the Dutch would mean we would be beholden to them in some regard, with an agreement of indentured servitude, perhaps, or at the least, beneath them always in standing. What we wanted was the King's charter and English financiers' investments so we could hire our own indentured servants and retain our English ways.

A year went by. Dorothy was pregnant. Her John was born. We smiled upon our children's play. Two more years passed. Our flowers were perennial, our gardens flourishing, our Dutch fluent. It seemed we would never leave Holland. I cannot say I was disappointed by this, but I do wonder how I am looking upon it now, with a more lavender hue than how it felt then.

Finally, the contracts were arranged, English financial backers secured, and the date for departure set.

This time, Dorothy's wish not to leave was even stronger. She had a full life—her friends, John's friends, the walks along the canal, the trips to the market, the farmer who performed for John a magic trick each time he saw him. Her loyalty to her husband outweighed her own desires, but now there was John. William said they would send for him once the colony was settled. It was too dangerous to risk his life to the seamen's illness, or worse. We both agreed to leave our children behind.

We planned our sons' lives in Amsterdam, with our parents, while we made homes for them in the Virginia Colony. We thought it would be a few months until we saw them, maybe a season, but no longer. The ache of leaving them behind was more rooted in the body than our husbands could understand. We confirmed with one another, time and again, this was for our sons' safety, this was the very best decision. We had to love our children enough to leave them behind.

That was the plan, then, Virginia, though the *Mayflower* drifted much farther north. The elders chose Virginia because anything farther south was too close to the Spanish, and anything farther north was too close to the Dutch.

Once we got to the Virginia Colony, there would be indentured servants to manage, houses to build, fences to make, fields to tend, a whole community to establish. A woman cannot work quickly with three children at her feet, tugging on her dress, calling, *Mum*. And there was the seamen's illness, which weakened adults and not much was known of what it did to children—we were to be one of the first group of English families to journey across the Atlantic. But even if the illness did not claim our sons and the servants were companionable and the strangers left us to our worship, as long as we kept quiet about it, as the King assured us we should, there were the Indians beyond the colony's fences, the stories of bloody battles.

I had seen an Indian once, displayed by the King in the courtyard of the Tower of London. There, betwixt the peacocks and flamingoes, past the birds of paradise, and a caged lion, the Indian stood, chains around both ankles, his hair pulled back behind him. The headdress they had him wearing fell sideways over his eyes, and his hands were somehow inaccessible, but how I could not tell. He was the tallest person I had ever seen. His eyes looked frightened, and then, as curious pale-skinned people got closer to him, his expression moved out past the English garden, past the peacocks, past it all, a stare that seemed to travel continents. He did not look ferocious. People said ungodly things to him, speaking as if he were more animal than human. I was struck by how the stories I'd heard of the Savages did not match his presence. It was like the one time I saw the Queen passing through our village, in her carriage, and I thought, *She is so small and ordinary*. Often things are more devious in our imagination by their distance to us.

But though I had seen that one Indian, that did not mean I was not scared of them. I heard there were thousands, this was a land of them, and how far they stretched and what pathways they made through forests were expansive. Later, once settled in Plymouth, I came to be thankful for the kindness of the Wampanoag Indians, for it was on their land we built.

We were to leave for Virginia in June in the year of our Lord sixteen hundred and twenty. We had our homes to sell, our heifers and bulls to disperse, possessions to evaluate. *Bring only the essential*, we were told, but Susanna White commissioned a wicker bassinet for her child that was not born yet. How hopeful it was, some women thought, and others, like me, thought it was inviting God's wrath to be that presumptuous.

I wonder what a difference it would have made to Dorothy if John had been on the *Mayflower*.

I remember her face on the day we were to leave for the Virginia Colony. Dorothy, on a rented horse, watching my sons emerge from the boardinghouse behind me. Her kind, dutiful face registering that though I said I would leave Constant and Thomas, though I gossiped with her in church about the women—including Mary and Susanna—who did not love their children enough to leave them behind, here I was, walking toward the carriage, bringing my sons with me, too. I could not do what I had promised, while she had left John that morning with her mother.

No room, I thought I saw Dorothy mouth to William.

He gave her a look, turned to me, and said, *Good morning*.

When I asked if this was possible, when I looked at him through my wobbly eyes—the tears—he said we would find a way, that there would be room for them.

Constant and Thomas trailed behind me, hands full with their belongings. I could not look her in the eyes. As we climbed in the back of the carriage I felt the heat of her stare like a heavy blanket I had not strength enough to lift. I deserved that look. The horses kicked up dirt and galloped down toward the dock.

At the dock, we stood together staring at the ship before us. Me with Constant and Thomas, Dorothy with her trunk and her husband's hand. Every person is a mystery and she was no exception. I thought she would miss John and say so, but if she grieved, the only sign was in the stiffness of her posture. Our friendship was shifting.

We watched a man step out of the Master's quarters. Bony, with oil-slick hair and large teeth, scowling at either the ship or the passengers below it. As unkempt as the least reputable.

Dorothy said, *Please, God, let this man not be the ship's Master.*

But he was the ship's Master.

I was hopeful Dorothy had forgiven me. I put my arm around her. Constant ran toward the edge, Thomas hung on Dorothy's hem, and before we knew it, without the reverence of ceremony, we were guided like cattle down into the dark tween deck, with the other women and children. We were not tall women, but still we had to bend our heads low to make our way across the closed-up space betwixt the storage below and the top deck above, a cabin of wood on all sides. We were the first human cargo to ride this *Speedwell*, which still smelled sweetly of the wine it had last imported. The journey from Delfshaven to London would take three days. Our *Speedwell* would meet with another ship, the *Mayflower*, in England, full of the strangers we needed to make the colony run— servants, carpenters, blacksmiths, farmers.

William could be heard ashore, giving a speech.

Do you want to go listen? I asked, pointing toward the ladder.

Dorothy smiled and said, *I heard it twice last night.*

I strained to hear William's words.

All the great and honorable actions are accompanied with great difficulties and must be enterprised and overcome with answerable courages . . . In our hearts we are pilgrims.

Our gathered brethren cheered.

It was light then, this future, because it was still new. I wanted to apologize, to acknowledge my advantage— Thomas and Constant—but I did not. I did not know how to say I was sorry. I did not want to press a bruise. That is what I told myself, but I see now I was too cowardly.

I had a cabin and so did Dorothy. They were called cabins by our husbands, and when we first inquired of the sleeping quarters and they said cabins, we imagined walls. We imagined privacy. Our *cabin* was a bed lifted off the floor, as high as our knees. We would fashion a little curtain with some scraps, but that was all. The chamber pot went beneath.

We watched a goat piss in front of us. The urine rolled along the grooved boards, cascaded over our belongings in the deck below.

Well, Dorothy said.

But it was just us congregates then, thirty-five of us combined in language and belief, where our similarities were a shorthand for comfort. The chickens and the children squawked. My sons inched closer to the barrels of gunpowder. I scanned the room and thought of all the ways I would be saying no to them for weeks.

We were half a day out of Holland when the ship's Master called down, *She leaks*. We both looked to the walls. They perspired. He said we would dock in Southampton that afternoon and might need to stay longer for repairs.

William thought the ship's Master was not to be trusted. We all did, but Dorothy said, with faith I could not muster, *It will be God's way*. I considered my own children and how to get them up the ladder and off the ship before the others if the ocean water rushed in. If the *Speedwell* were to sink, I was not willing to leave their lives to God's way. I apologized to God for this transgression, yet there it was and there I was again, sinning.

When we docked, what I remember of Southampton is the glitter of the sun on a dull sea. The town's better days had been years ago. As is a monarch's way, King James called Southampton the finest and sweetest in the kingdom. But when the town declined after losing its monopoly on transporting tin, he quickly sold the castle. The town walls were weedy with elder and yew. Nature asserts where man no longer claims it. On a hill, under the castle keep, a butcher chased after a pig. Another man with a bloody apron ran his hand along a cow's spine.

Seamen from other ships were in circles on the dock when we arrived, gambling. I smelled dead fish. I heard a lute. Even in this place, the summer conspired toward celebration. Down toward the dock came Thomas Weston to greet us. Where were my sons? One held Dorothy's hand, one held mine.

We moved closer into town. Darkness grew. There were jeers from the alehouses, seamen moving out into the alleyways, their voices gaining in volume. The glint of knives. Women in doorsteps, with one knee lifted, giving a soft hello to our husbands. We scowled at them. We hooked arms around one another. I picked up Thomas. He grew heavy—*God tests!*—but the day's excitement had him asleep before we reached the boardinghouse. My husband outstretched his arms and took him. It was one of the last movements of strength I saw in my husband in this lifetime.

The boardinghouse was not ready for us. We had missed dinner, John Carver said, and William disagreed. Through the hallway we saw guests, portly men dressed for business, wiping their plates clean with biscuits, guests stepping up from their chairs, brushing the crumbs from their laps, and finishing the dregs of the wine. Had the innkeeper eyed us and decided not to feed us because we were exiles?

I understood suspicion. It should have been a relief for us to be in a country that spoke our language, but then, one feels worse for how close it appears we should be but are not. Those English-speakers were not our brethren. Who was against us? Who agreed with the King's call to rid us—so-called puritans—out of England, or bring back our heads to, as the King said, *Punish their traitorous nature?*

Puritans, I thought I heard.

Did you hear that? I asked Dorothy.

Yes, she had.

We were back in England's scorn. I had forgotten what that felt like.

We were wearing the styles of a decade ago, when last we were in England. It was vain to be concerned with these things, but better if one is to be vain, to be vain together with a friend, to share the burden.

Are we not paying guests as the rest? William inquired to the innkeeper.

John Carver, one of the wealthiest amongst us, offered money. The biscuits arrived. We took the children upstairs to sleep. I told Dorothy my husband was not well, had not been in the weeks leading up to this journey. A cough that would not cease, a wakefulness in the night even after a day's long labor.

He'll be fine once we get settled into the ship's distance, she said.

Cold was its comfort.

William knocked on the door, to show Dorothy to their room. She kissed my forehead before leaving. I can still smell the myrrh that perfumed her hair.

That night, I woke to my husband hunched over the side of the bed, trying to get his breath. I moved toward him, put my palm to his back, and felt the bones along his spine. I lightly beat my fists against his back to move the fluid about.

I'm fine, Good Wife, he said, wanting to usher me back to sleep, without worry for him. He was this way, too austere toward himself. It was only a cough, he said. I had not been one to worry too soon, and needlessly, before this, but long after his deep breath of sleep returned, my eyes were open.

I had not thought on it much, his age and, subsequently, his death. That he was a decade and a half older than I and would likely leave this earthly world before me was only an idea. People perished all of the time—whole villages fell to plague—but never did I think of how this death would come for us. How foolish I was.

The day's matrimonial annoyances—that he kicked our sons' jacks under the chair rather than pick them up and return them to their place—were not worth the effort I expended on the feeling. Edward Southworth, my Good Husband, might die. I would be a widow with two small children. Where would I go? Who would help me? I tried to conjure there, in that boardinghouse room, everything I loved about Edward. When in the midst of a life with young children, the mind strains to remember our spouses' goodness, despite how often we address each other as *Good Wife* and *Good Husband*. I thought of Edward whistling through the house, of Edward lifting Constant off the ground, of Edward taking my hand unexpectedly while I cooked, stopping me to say, *I love you, Good Wife.*

I can see now this was God's warning. He came that night to prepare me. My husband would pass long before me and what would I do?

There I was on that lumpy borrowed bed, crying for my husband, who was right there beside me, breathing, his eyes fluttering in dream.

What we thought would be one night, maybe two, at the boardinghouse, waiting on the ship's repair, expanded into several weeks without signs of an impending departure. Our tab to the port of Southampton grew. William took morning walks to the dock and found the ship's Master playing cards, throwing dice, the whiff of evening still on him. Perhaps the Master got a cut of the port fee and that was why he was in no hurry to leave. William had no trust in that ship's Master. It was no secret William was angry, but when I gave Dorothy the entryway to speak on it—*William must be disappointed*, I would say— she nodded and kept William's thoughts to herself.

Each day docked in Southampton added the cost of more rooms for thirty-five people at the boardinghouses, and each afternoon when it was clear we would not depart, William took an item from the larder. We lost several pounds of butter. We lost many salted fish.

William wrote letters back to London, pleading to our debtors.

Dear Sirs, he wrote, *We were in such a strait as we were forced to sell sixty pounds of our provisions to clear our debts, and now we are scarce of butter, with no oil to mend a shoe, lacking swords and in want of muskets.* But a complaint by William would never turn to self-pity, would it? At the end of each letter he affirmed God's good grace. *And yet, we are willing to expose ourselves to such eminent dangers and put our trust in God . . . Faith will be the staple food of our journey.*

On the Sabbath the women of the congregation left the boardinghouse to sing Psalms in a loud chorus in front of the alehouse, to outshine the raucous. This chorus was led by Susanna White, and with her protruding belly, I imagine even the most ungodly of the seamen subdued their anger at the women's righteousness.

We had to sell so much butter.

At this rate, we'll be as thin as poppies, Dorothy said.

I thought of the little bobbing heads of us as girls, in the old days gathering flowers, getting them ready for sale at the market, and when our mothers were not watching, lying around amidst them, brushing the pollen off of one another's backs.

Two weeks went by this way, us losing butter for our future, seeds for our future, a goat for our future. Dorothy sold her mother's horn clip. I thought my pregnancy days were over, and sold the wicker bassinet. I did not wish to risk my life in labor once again, and Edward and I were no longer frequent with our intimacies.

But I did not know then what Dorothy did in secret, in the mornings, when no one else was watching. In Southampton, she sent her mother a letter. A short letter paid for on credit, on our congregation's tab.

Dear Mother. Please. Help me return. William will not be persuaded.

Dorothy's mother confessed to me she never wrote a reply. I told her it was not her fault, I told her it must have been an accident, I told her all the things that were told to me, because I'm no longer certain one needs to carry the burden of some truths.

We departed Southampton, but within a day we were docked again, this time at Plymouth, the last port before entering the Atlantic. On another dock, on another shore, not even out of the English Channel.

Perhaps this is a sign, I said to Dorothy.

Again she said, *He tests.*

Was she suffering privately? What did she share with William? I noticed he was gentle with her, coming up behind her saying, *My Good Wife,* and *Good Mother,* the highest honors, not stingy with his affection. I wondered if *Good Mother* caused her to wince, inwardly. John and her unnamed daughter growing farther and farther away.

I looked behind to my husband, who had just stepped above deck. He was getting weaker, I saw, but hadn't lost his spirit. Though from my husband's expression— quizzical, questioning of all that surrounded us—I sensed I would betray Dorothy.

What followed were four days more paying port fees, boardinghouse fees, meals for all of us, more debt, more debt. William never slept well, Dorothy said, and I saw him often, walking alone down the cobblestone streets, the first to walk into the wind and rain and the last to leave it.

She leaks, she leaks, is all that the ship's Master said, or all, at least, that was reported back to us.

Perhaps this was a scheme to make the bill higher, to owe the investors in England even more money and increase their profit.

We congregates gathered around the boardinghouse table, dipping bread into potato soup, the husbands considering our choices. To combine ships or find another Master. Constant would not eat despite—or more likely, because of—my encouragement. I kept trying to keep up my son's strength as I watched my husband's lessen. My husband claimed the previous breakfast had still left him quite full and declined more than a bird's portion.

William said, about the ship's accountant, *I saw him return to the ship this morning with what must be a hundred or more pounds of provisions.*

Heads turned, ears cocked. He waited for this attention before he continued.

That's our money, Standish said.

William continued: *I asked him, "What is all this?" and like the scoundrel I'm now convinced he is, he refused to show me the accounting.*

We each imagined he had purchased what we longed for most. Goose fat, gimlet, a pick axe, what had the accountant tucked away, unnoticed? Why had he come back with a hundred pounds' worth of provisions, which he had the seamen put in the berth and refused to discuss the contents or accounting with any of us?

The families began to retire to bed, and I myself was going to lead my sons upstairs, when both the Master of the *Speedwell* and the Master of the *Mayflower* entered the boardinghouse. They had conferred, they said, and it was resolved. The *Speedwell* would not continue across the Atlantic. At this news, Myles Standish stood. William was already standing.

I cannot do more, the *Speedwell*'s Master said. *She leaks.*

If we were to go to the Virginia Colony, we would all have to fit on the *Mayflower*, which was full as it was with our indentured servants and adventurers who were strangers to us. The ship was bursting with four dozen passengers, and there were three dozen more of us. We had to choose amongst ourselves who would go and who would stay behind. A ranking was beginning amongst the elders, of which men brought the most to the colony, an ordering of wealth and ableness.

My husband put his hand on my shoulder.

Good Wife, shall we? he asked.

We went upstairs. Instead of speaking to Dorothy about all of this, I spoke that night to Edward. We waited for our sons to be softly snoring in the bed betwixt us.

It was September. Westerly gales were building across the Atlantic. He was not well, he said. By sunrise it was decided: When the ship departed, my husband and I would step out of line.

Dorothy was not downstairs in the morning. The innkeeper said she and William had since departed. I hurried to gather my sons and get to the dock. My husband shooed us onward, said he would catch up.

Through the boardinghouse's back garden I went, Constant and Thomas slow behind me, so very slow, stopping to watch a snail, to touch the dewy roses I warned them not to touch. It was in this way, me moving forward, then turning back to urge them onward, that I stepped on something that slithered beneath my right foot. I shrieked. There it was, an iridescent green snake, a sign from God, maintaining its place on the limestone.

What is it? Constant yelled, running in delight toward whatever curious thing had terrified his mother.

Nothing, I said, knowing they would traipse through the ivy to find it and I needed to get to Dorothy.

The serpent moved away, I said, but my sons did not believe me.

I got them to the dock with the threat that I would pinch their ears the entire walk there if I needed to. The serpent had marked me.

At the dock, Dorothy had an upright posture and looked out on the water. The white ribbon of her bonnet blew out to the side, and her aubergine dress blew outward with it. She began to cross onto the ship.

I told the boys not to move an inch. Their father was a few paces behind, close enough, I wagered, to disrupt any mischief they might cause. I hurried up the ramp, onto the *Mayflower*, and down the ladder into the tween deck. So dark it was and musty. I felt a moment of relief knowing I would not be on this journey.

I found Dorothy setting down her basket. I took her hand in mine. I furrowed my face, preparing my apology, which I knew would be inadequate.

Dorothy stopped me, said, *I wish—*

What? I asked, but I knew what was happening. Each time she thought of a way to tell William she should turn back she answered with his reply before she spoke it.

So many people were nearby and would have overheard her speaking against her husband. Her placid face, her sweet, unwavering face, took in my apology before I said it, and, I'd like to think, accepted it, hugging me and wishing me well.

We will join one another soon enough, she said.

She gave me her handkerchief. Why had I not thought to bring her anything? I felt myself an inconsiderate friend and said so. I looked in her eyes longer than I had done in years and said we would see one another very soon. But I was not certain.

On the way up, William's arm brushed against mine. I looked up to see him. I felt aware of the warmth where our arms touched. My husband had spoken to him on the dock, but I did not know that at the time.

You will be missed, he said and looked down to me.

He bent down and embraced me. So close I was to his lips. I gave him a kiss on the cheek and moved quickly back up the ladder, tripping on a rung as I went.

On the dock was my sanguine husband, holding Thomas's hand.

You will miss your friend, he said, seeing my failed composure.

I nodded.

We waved then to the ship, to all our friends in the tween deck, to the young boys nervous to be at sea, to the older, indifferent sorts, and to the wizened seamen above. Blessings were called and the hope that those below could hear us.

Thus, that common merchant ship, named not for primrose, cuckooflower, marigold, or cowslip, but for anything that could flower in May, pushed out to the sea.

My husband, our sons, and I walked slowly back to the boardinghouse. We intended to return to Holland as soon as passage could be booked. But by the end of the week, my husband was dead.

I won't speak of my journey back to Holland, a widow with two young sons and no means to care for them. Numb, I was, in spirit. God cares for us by selecting some things for us to forget. I sold most of our possessions—my husband's boots, a musket, candlesticks, two chairs—which we had intended to take to the New World, in order to pay for our return.

The children and I took up residence with my parents. I woke each morning with two grieving boys. Dorothy, my dearest consort, moved an ocean away and my husband was dead. This was not the life I thought would be mine. In the mornings I set myself in mind to get to my friend as soon as I could, but by afternoon it was all I could do to chase a chicken around the yard as my sons napped, and pluck its feathers before they awoke. I tried to feed them well if nothing else. No food comforted me. My body thinned as only before when I grew rapidly in youth. *How does a person live with this weight of sadness?* I thought then. The answer, I see now, is simple: One just does. Until one cannot.

Meanwhile

Meanwhile, in Plymouth, an indentured servant, thirteen years of age, lies on the floor, on a bed of wool, next to her master's bed, as she does every night. Meanwhile, at the edge of the bed is not her master's wife, but her master's brother. She startles awake at the feeling of his hand beneath her blanket.

Shhh, he whispers. *You do not want to wake your master, do you?*

She turns from him.

He rolls her over.

Do what I say, good servant.

He slides off the edge of the bed and climbs onto her. He wrestles her linens away from her body.

She is stiff.

That's a good girl. It will be easier this way, he says.

No one has touched her, aside from her grandmother and her mother, when they bathed her and put talcum powder betwixt her legs as a younger child. He pulls up her long nightdress, he inserts a thick finger in her cunny. His fingernails are long.

He shifts out of his linens. A warm, stiff thing in the dark pushes against her.

He is stiff and remote, grating inside her, squeezing her right breast like a cow's udder, but with less precision— he's never lowered himself to milking a cow—and like the animal he is he lets out a guttural *Oh*. He shifts up his linens, leaves her naked, and slides back to the bed above her.

From across the room, the mistress of the house stirs. She does not know if the mistress is or was awake.

Had she done or said anything to him to invite this? The way she bowed? The way she smiled? Was she untoward?

Her master's brother whispers, *If you speak thus, no one would believe you. You would be tried for slanderous speech.*

She says nothing.

You love your sister, don't you?

She says nothing.

If you tell anyone, I will kill her.

She sees he is not lying. He is capable of killing.

Meanwhile, she tells no one until nine months later, when she has a daughter of her own. The elders come for her, accuse her of lying with a man before betrothal.

At her trial the judge asks, *And why, if he did what you said he did, why did you not tell your master at once?*

As if delay were not a sign of shock, as if delay were not proof of indignity, but instead a sign of embellishment. She transfers houses. Her daughter grows strong. The master's brother is acquitted and returns on occasion to Plymouth. A new servant girl takes her place.

Who is this woman? Any woman. Meanwhile, meanwhile, meanwhile.

Alice Bradford

There was so much I did not notice on that day, such as the growing tensions within the colony and the anger toward my husband by those estranged from God. Instead, I wanted to read what my husband had written.

Joseph was asleep on my breast, his mouth slightly open. Now was my chance. I laid him on the bed next to Mercy, who had, to my good fortune, fallen asleep on her own. I went back to the desk.

I lifted the papers. I had never seen that leather-bound before. What a husband wishes to keep hidden, a wife knows well enough not to pursue. I opened the book. *Of Plymouth Plantation. 1620*, it said, and in William's penmanship, *In their hearts, they were pilgrims.*

I read and turned pages for far longer than I knew was right, which made it, I confess, more enjoyable. The story of us. Not I and him, but of us believers, in Holland, and the *Mayflower* journey, and the last ten years here. In vanity I looked for myself, but I was not there. And after myself, I looked for Dorothy. I went back to the pages of the *Mayflower*. The lascivious seaman who wished to throw them overboard was there, and his death was told as God's punishment for how he treated them. The cracked timber that nearly killed them all was there, and was told as God's test and subsequent rainbow. All the deaths aboard the ship and all the deaths that first winter were there, except the death of her, his first wife, my dearest consort, Dorothy May Bradford. Why does our love pass by some bodies but still at others? Anything we say about love we say as an absence.

There were other things, too, that William did not speak of. No mention of the footpaths and graves. The small child buried with a beaded bracelet and leather shoes, next to a full-grown man with long blond hair still attached to his skull. William scarcely mentioned how we buried our dead and did not say that in the worst of times, that first winter, we propped our dead Englishmen against the trees at the edges of our colony, with muskets, to make it seem as if we had soldiers amongst us, a forest sentinel, and not the truth: that we had lost more than half of our people.

I went out to do the washing and left the door ajar to listen for the children. Something in me had been stirred. That smell, that absence. I needed fresh air. It was this distraction, perhaps, that blinded me from seeing the signs of what was to come later that afternoon.

Part Two

Newcomen

Newcomen was not pleased with his interaction with John Billington.

He went to Standish's post. Standish's servant was sitting on an overturned bucket, whittling, and did not look up when Newcomen spoke.

Left for Duxbury. He's got land there.

John looked up at a blood-splattered sheet flying above them both.

The servant shrugged. *Looking for a quieter way of life*, he said.

Newcomen thanked him and started over to the meetinghouse, to see what the women had cooked. He did not want to ask for much, but he needed sustenance to help him through the rest of the day.

Newcomen had been looking for quiet, too, but Captain Standish had put him next to what he suspected was the town's most difficult man. Newcomen tried not to muse too long on this, though, for he could easily linger on how men with power always took more for themselves, how men who have had nothing hoard what they have and take what is not theirs, how the world is a terrible place he was trying not to avoid. How this follows him everywhere, even to a town striving to be in God's favor.

John Newcomen saw Captain Standish approach the meetinghouse on a black horse. So he had not gone to Duxbury. Standish got down and tied her up to a post. Newcomen knew to take this moment to speak with Captain Standish alone before the passengers on the boat out at sea, arriving within hours, would occupy his time by inquiring about their land.

The acreage, Newcomen said, *abutting the Billingtons?*

Yes. Standish took off his black gloves, exposing his long, pale fingers. Fingers too pristine for the type of work building a colony required.

Where doth it begin?

At the oak, as I showed you.

Perhaps another plot is available?

I'm afraid not, Standish said.

Why had he, John Newcomen, been so vain as to want for more than England?

For Eugenia. For his mother. For himself.

John thanked Standish for the kindness he had not shown him, lowered his head, and stepped into the meetinghouse.

Alice Bradford

From the chest I pulled a blue and yellow blanket, one I believed to have been John's. I kept it at the bottom of the chest, despite all need for any warmth, because I wanted it to be as close to how he remembered it. I shook it high in the air and watched the dust motes fall like tiny stars.

I pulled out the trundle bed and placed Joseph atop it, then lifted the blanket off quickly.

Where is Joseph?

There you are.

That game that delights all children.

Mercy nudged her way betwixt us, wanting the attention I was giving to her brother.

Before I could admonish her, there was a knock on the door and then the door burst open. It was Susanna.

It's here! Susanna said.

They are here! Elizabeth said, coming in behind her. She looked at both of us and ran out, leaving the door open.

We all rushed outside. The pounding of hammers on the roofs had stopped. The light was fragile and the air felt that way, too. There was the boat, so ordinary, so small, carrying so many wishes. I started running.

Watch them? I called to Elizabeth.

She gave a put-out face, but stepped back into my gardens.

Susanna and I broke into a run, like girls, through the path, not the forty-year-old women that we were. Though my innards were as delicate as cheesecloth from birthing Joseph, and she was nearing the end of her pregnancy, still, we ran. We let the momentum and wind surge us toward the dock.

The ship lay anchor. I hoped the new colonists would be stronger and more pious than the last.

The first heads to pop up from the tween deck were small black-capped men. Then came three heifers and a bull and behind them, more men, half a dozen women, and with them a handful of children. There they were, four dozen or so, sickly and sea-legged. Their pale English bodies, weakened by the journey, as if ghosts, crossing over. One by one, the women's bare ankles and leather shoes dipped in the surfaces of the sea. I knew their look well—their hopeful and fearful imaginations of the present situation.

They stepped ashore, many of them likely harboring the seamen's illnesses, and it would be our women's work to lay them down, put wet cloths upon their heads, wash their clothes, feed them broth, and assure them they would not die. Though some likely would.

Where was John? Was he the one with his head down, coughing? Was he the sturdy one holding the rope of a large black cow? It had been seven years—I doubted I would know him.

On shore, William walked forward, then back. For each person who stepped across the water, he put one arm on their shoulder, and shook the other. Welcoming, he was. Tall and strong, wearing his most open face.

But not three feet away from him was John Billington. Billington crossed his arms and smirked, ready, it seemed, to counter all of Governor Bradford's enthusiasm. In the middle, but behind them, was Captain Standish.

I saw a man wearing the tallest starched white collar of ruffles that I had ever seen.

Who is that? I asked Susanna.

Those ruffles? Some London fool.

I squinted and looked closer. When he took off his hat to greet my husband, I saw that I did know this man. It was Thomas Weston.

I did not think William was expecting *the* Thomas Weston himself, the financial backer who had arranged the *Mayflower* journey. The one I thought had colluded with pirates on our last shipment back to London. The way he shook my husband's hand confirmed it. Not only had a representative been sent to check up on us, their investment, but he'd also been sent to evaluate my husband.

Master Weston, I heard William say.

William used more force than usual, putting his other hand over the handshake.

Thick was the musk perfume around Master Weston, denying the smell of the human body God granted him. He was trying to disguise himself as God disapproved.

Susanna and I watched more men depart the ship, cross the water, and step onto the shore. I scanned for Dorothy's son, looking to see a chin I recognized, a smile I remembered. I looked to John Billington, wondering what he would do.

When he, too, saw that it was Thomas Weston, John Billington stepped forward.

Well, if it isn't the biggest liar in all of England.

Though his voice was loud, Weston did not hear him, or feigned not hearing him.

Ah, 'tis good to be among friends, Thomas Weston said, patting my husband's back.

My husband led him up the hill, away from John Billington.

I had known Thomas Weston for two decades, but he was nearly unrecognizable to me. When he was an iron-monger marrying my friend Mary, he seemed like one of us, transporting Elder Brewster's pamphlets against the King to London, passing our dissenting voice back to those who needed it. My husband had trusted Weston enough to have him procure the investors for our venture. But those ruffles were an outward sign of his inner fall.

He had traded in children and lied to us about their origins. For the *Mayflower* journey ten years ago, he asked the congregates to take along four orphaned siblings. Weston claimed they were brought to him by their uncle, Lord Zouche, who offered a healthy sum to *give them a second chance at the godly way*. The eldest, Ellen More, was eight and the youngest girl, four. All but one died before that first winter was over. At the death of the second youngest, Jasper, on the *Mayflower*, Ellen told a different story. She said both her parents were very much alive.

Why are you here, then? Susanna asked her.

Ellen said it was the neighbor who was her father.

Had we known these men were separating a mother from her children, I like to think we might not have agreed to take them.

So as one could see, Thomas Weston was a man who cared not how he earned a profit, only that he got it. Seeing his untrustworthy face again, I was certain he hired those pirates to take our profits. If he had ever been in the godly way, it was easy to look at those ruffles now and see how far he had strayed. His shirt's collar was as high as his ears and his nose was high in the air—as it had to be to hold up such a grand artifice.

Susanna clucked her tongue. She said, *Ah, the new rich, having nothing else in them but a few fine clothes.*

When the men passed, I pressed down my bonnet and tucked the stray hair behind my ear.

Good day, madam, one said.

So it was, I was a madam. I had not grown accustomed to it, *madam* over *miss*. Yet another vanity of mine, for which I apologized to God. The young men meant it in respect, they did, and yet each time I heard it I thought to look behind myself, to where a madam might be standing. In our hearts, we madams would always be misses.

I smiled and returned the pleasantries. I wished I blushed—an outward sign of inward modesty—but I did not.

I heard a whoop and a cheer and someone calling, *Johnny Boy!*

Master Billington squinted, raised his hand, smiled, and loped over to a man I did not initially recognize. He was tall and aristocratic—his cloak had metal buttons and he wore a tall black hat. The two laughed and slapped backs.

Oh no! I thought, suddenly recognizing him.

It was Thomas Morton, that Lord of Misrule, whom my husband had banished from the colony two years prior. Thomas Morton, who oversaw the trading outpost in Merrymount, but had led the ungodly among us to trade with the Indians and drink to excess. Thomas Morton who persuaded men and women to shed their clothes, whereupon they lay with one another openly. My husband had complained, before Morton's banishment, *All the scum of the country flock to him.*

How had he gotten passage on this boat and returned? I would have to wait until speaking with William privately to find out.

The last to exit the ship was a young man with a gait like William. His head down, feet sturdy, slow. When he got close enough, I took his hand.

It was a soft hand, a lithe hand. He was twelve years old and approaching the height of his father. In his eyes was Dorothy.

Welcome home, I said. *Let me show you the way.*

John Billington

When the bell sounded the ship's arrival, John Billington went with the rest. There was no one he was expecting, no one he knew on the ship, but it was customary and polite to greet new people.

The whole town came out. When John Billington first stepped off the *Mayflower* and onto the shore, he had been greeted only by the whir of cold November winds. No fire or alehouse or friends. After the solemnness of their long journey, these newcomers must be met.

To his surprise, out of the berth of the ship he saw Thomas Morton emerge.

I thought they'd killed you! And now here they are, letting you back?

The two men embraced.

If one pays enough . . .

Thomas Morton let that linger, smiled the secret smile of two old friends.

Come, let's have a drink, said John Billington, and they went onward to Billington's house.

Alice Bradford

I was at the fire, stirring the pot of stew I would take to the dinner, when in the house came my stepson, squinting, with the ax. It was just us.

When would be the right time? I had not yet spoken of Dorothy to him, and with the business of the newcomers, I might not speak to him much at all the rest of the evening. I did not want the weight of her upon me.

Your mother, I said.

He put down the ax.

She loved you so very much, I said.

Why did I not look at him? So little time there is on this earth.

He moved toward me. I heard his feet, then heard them stop.

My grandmum said she slipped, he said.

In his tone was the question. The wonder if it was true. The question I had been asking myself for years.

Who was I to tell him any differently? What good would it do him?

I turned to him.

I'm sorry she is not here to see you, to see you now.

Yes, he said and looked away to a corner of the room.

A painting taken from her home in Leiden was on the wall. William thought it had come from the market. But it had been a gift from Johannes.

I remember that, John said, pointing to it.

He looked to the pottery, too.

He glided his hand along the ledge.

I only wanted to eat from this plate. Father said no, that she was indulging me. She would scoop off her own food to put mine upon it. I wish I hadn't asked for that.

You were a child, I said. It was too soon for me to say: *Children take as much as mothers will give them.* I would save that for when he had children himself. It was too soon to say, *It is their way, to test their mother's devotion.*

I heard William's boots kick against the house. A sound I loved. The stew was ready, the bread was fresh, and the fire was strong. We would be a family. We were a family.

Eleanor Billington

It was a welcoming surprise to see Tom on that ship and be again amongst friends. He came back to our house for a drink and caught us up on a manuscript he was writing, *The New English Canaan*, which railed against the hypocrisy of Plymouth.

Quoted ye, I did, said Tom to my husband.

What did ye say?

How you spoke for the people and were punished for it. How these Plymouth leaders are more Savage than the so-called Savages.

Tom spoke some of it to us.

He wrote of how the Algonquins he knew could tell a Spaniard from a Frenchman by the smell of their hands, how they behaved as landed gentry—moving from the seacoast inward with the weather, fishing and hunting with the seasons, living as free and leisurely as the well-born British, with their idle pleasures—but that the puritans would never acknowledge the comparison.

Thomas Morton had much to say and we had much to complain about. Even from the beginning those hypocrites fashioned themselves quite differently from what they were. It was with help from the Wampanoag Indians that the Englishmen of Plymouth flourished.

While back in London, Morton went to the house of Sir Ferdinando Gorges. He told us of two Indians he kept captive there.

Purchased in Malaga, and Gorges said, as if Jesus himself, "Saved them from slavery, I did." Called them "His wonders."

And they wonder why your trading post was the most successful, said I.

No person wants to be thought of as less than human. Tom was a man of wealth. He had little that he could lose, except his life, which is no small thing, but at the time, seemed worth the risk. We clinked our goblets and cheered his truth-telling.

One drink turned to three. Had my husband and Tom Morton not been imbibing on an empty stomach before dinner and instead gone out to the fields, I am certain the evening would not have taken the turn it did.

A bell rang through the colony, announcing dinner.

Tom said, *Ah, we have not yet gotten dinner.*

I had the meat pie on the table and offered it.

Go on, my husband said to Tom, *make merry at the meetinghouse.*

What he meant was, make trouble. My husband hated the hypocrites, but did not want to tell Tom we were not invited to dinner.

Tom smiled. *I cannot miss the opportunity to see them squirm.* He patted my husband's shoulder, stood, and said, *I shall join you after.*

Tom slid a flask from his cloak and slipped it to my husband. *Just the thing to celebrate with when I get back,* Tom said, and walked out the door to the meetinghouse.

My husband took a long sip, then brought down his musket from the wall.

Where are ye going with the gun, John?

The woods, he said.

Going to shoot some hypocrites? I said. It was a joke.

Tomorrow. Tonight, deer.

But I have pie.

He had set his mind on deer, though, and would not be persuaded otherwise.

A bit late for that, I called, as he walked away from the house.

John Billington

It would be hours before his dinner if he wished for deer, but that was his wish, and so few of them went fulfilled that he would allow this one. His stomach ached, shrunk inward by the eight hours he had gone without.

He came upon the crowd forming on the two roads to the meetinghouse. All those hypocrites, smiling and laughing, their bellies soon to be full. The smell of venison wafted over to him.

You have it nicely here, don't you, Master Billington? said a voice behind him.

John Billington turned to see Thomas Weston. Weston was a compact man and the errant white strands of hair were one of the few things that revealed his age. His chin jutted out, which gave the impression of being slightly perturbed, a physical feature that benefited him in negotiation.

Your letter caused quite the stir amongst investors.

John Billington let the barrel of his gun touch the ground and leaned against it. The drinks with Tom had left him more unsteady than he realized. He paused before replying.

We signed away seven years to be in Virginia, amongst English people. Not these devils, disguising themselves as devout.

You are a landowner, are you not, Master Billington?

John Billington looked away.

Quite a step up from London, eh? There you'd be in debtors' prison or more likely dead. If I were you I would count your blessings.

You know what you promised us.

So you want me to take you back?

John Billington shifted his weight off of his gun.

As I am sure you know, Master Weston, Bradford burned down Morton's house. For trading fur better than he could. Of course Bradford lied and blamed the house-burning on Morton's merrymaking. Hypocrites, murdering and destroying property as it suits them. Sundays here you would think the town had the plague.

Weston was smiling.

Are you saying you wish to sell your land and go back to London, Master Billington?

You knew they were going to take us north, not to Virginia.

I agree it is not fertile land, won't get you much, but if you need it taken off your hands . . . Might pay for you and your family to return.

For the work I've done here, you should have paid me. My son dead.

John Billington was not keeping the promise he made with himself to stop letting these people bother him.

My whole family nearly died, and you've yet to acknowledge your lies. Sold those children to those hypocrites. Two years old, that youngest. You'll do anything for a profit, but what will a profit do for you in the afterlife, Master Weston?

If Billington's claims had an effect on Weston, no one observing Weston could have seen it.

So you want me to take you back?

John Billington stared at Weston.

In a flat voice, Weston said, *What do you want.* It was not a question.

Billington adjusted the weight of his gun.

You know what I want. I've said it.

Myles Standish stood in the doorway of the meetinghouse. The crowd was filing inside. Thomas Weston looked over to him.

What I want, Master Weston, is an admission and an apology. Tell the truth and be absolved from your sins. You knew where you were sending us.

Dinner, Standish called to Weston, his voice a little higher than usual. He did not set his eyes upon Billington.

As if Billington had not spoken, Thomas Weston said, *Good day, Master Billington,* and started toward the meetinghouse.

You are a lying rascal and a rogue, Thomas Weston, Billington called out.

Weston turned. He walked back to Billington and only stopped when he was close enough to bite Billington's ear.

Listen, you knave. I could have you dead by nightfall. No one here would know who did it and every single person in this colony would celebrate.

Weston adjusted his cuffs. *Nay, you are not worth the gunpowder it would take.*

Weston then called to Standish, *What have your fine women prepared for us?* and strode into the meetinghouse.

John Billington walked quickly past, tipped his hat to the guards, moved through the palisade, then out, at last, past Plymouth proper and in the open air of his property, where he could think.

Dumping out their shitty chamber pots, burying their dead, thatching their roofs before he had finished his own, had he not given them enough? Had he not done enough, for seven years as their servant? No, it seemed, he hadn't. He would always be a servant, always be the man—barely a man—they told what to do. Had he not tired his back and arms building their houses by day, then dragged himself to his small square of dirt and hammered at night on his own? Chopped their firewood, as they demanded, before his own, poured their beer before his own, ate only the table scraps they deigned to give him. Indentured servitude was stale bread and watery stew they fed him last. He had lost a stone that first year from the labor. It would have been better if more of them had died. He had risked, in caring for them, dying himself. Still they called him the most lascivious man, patriarch of the most profane family. Those precisionists believed in God's plan and though they claimed no one knew who God chose, who were His Elect, you could see it on their faces, how much they thought it was themselves, who were chosen, how much they thought God would never choose a man like himself, a John Billington. But maybe it was he who was chosen, if there were such a thing. Maybe it was him. God had not killed him, not yet, and wasn't that a sign of God's favor, Captain Shrimp? A sign of God's good grace, Governor Bradford? Billington kicked up a heavy stone with his boot. Nay, nay, he would always be below them.

He would go again to Standish. This evening, in front of the newcomers. He would demand Shrimp give him the land he was due.

Alice Bradford

For the evening meal, we gave the newcomers more food from the storehouse than we gave ourselves. The high oak beams of the meetinghouse were grand, I thought, in their simplicity. We women pushed the tables together for the occasion and decorated each with a pitcher of sweet goldenrod. We placed our venison pies, soft cheeses, salad herbs, corn meal boiled with dried peas, loaves of bread, and generous amounts of butter atop the tables.

My husband gave a speech, welcoming the newcomers. One butterfly followed the flowers into the room and fluttered around my husband as he spoke. I smiled at the kind of sign this could be.

And some, he said, *not so new*, and motioned to Thomas Morton.

The congregants in the crowd chuckled with unease. Morton smiled. Before dinner, back at home, my husband had voiced fury with Weston for bringing Thomas Morton back. Weston claimed he had not known of Morton's banishment.

Water under the bridge, Bradford. Give him another chance. As an Englishman, he does improve relations with the Indians, Weston had said.

Our elder, William Brewster, stood. He was our lay minster most of these past ten years, for we could not find a suitable priest for Plymouth.

Let us pray, he said, and bowed his head, leading us in a blessing of the food, and thankfulness to God's bounty, so that it might protect and nourish us.

I prayed, too, that these newcomers would not cause as much trouble as I feared they would. I was reminded again of what Pastor Robinson had said when my husband wrote to him proudly about the deaths of Massachusett men. *Once there is bloodshed, there will be more.* I wished he had not been right in this, as he so often was.

The Billingtons absence was unnoticed, or noticed only in its relief. I offered my new stepson a plate and ale before the other children. The seamen sat together at one table, hulking over their food, few with napkins over their shoulders. I thought of a boy and his mother I had seen on the dock before I boarded the *Anne*. The mother said, *Be of good courage,* and slipped a red cap upon his head. Her son loped off, new seaman that he was, and only then, privately, did she turn her head and wipe her tears away. Somebody loves us all. Not only God, but someone earthly, too. Or did, anyway. The seamen's uncouth ways were not, when thought of this way, a bother to me.

Weston had a seat next to my husband, and beside him, Elder Brewster, and then Susanna's husband. Thomas Morton and the seamen were already getting seconds of ale and meat before I had taken my first bite. The butter was down to slivers. We women ate together with the children, taking less than what our bellies wished for, hopeful some would be left over. There never was.

After their ale and with bellies warmed, and after my husband's prayer for what we had consumed, the men's laughter grew. I watched the dirty bowls pile up on tables not abandoned. In the center of the room the elders talked. I imagined they spoke of money. Debts. I perceived a growing tension at my husband's table by the way Elder Brewster's arms were folded. William had told me before dinner how few provisions Weston had brought over with the newcomers. I worried the state of our affairs was dire, but sitting there worrying would do nothing. There was a meetinghouse to clean. I took up three empty pitchers and asked the women who would like to join me. Elizabeth stood. I left Joseph sleeping in his Moses basket next to his father. Mercy and William the younger were amongst the other children—William playing jacks and Mercy twirling together stems of wild flowers. Elizabeth and I set out for the brook.

As safe as I felt in Plymouth, there was stillness in that path, and the sound of the water prevented me from hearing other sounds, which left me unsettled. Had I known what fates were being made there in the forest that night, I would have avoided the brook. The cleaning could have waited.

Nature

In summer, all that is green hushes that which is not. Sassafras bend their necks in the wind. A box turtle hatchling takes her first stride. A shrew makes a squeak only his kind can hear. A snake unhinges his jaw around the shrew. Three white-tailed deer graze in an open field, father, mother, and a child on wobbly legs.

There is the flora and there is the fauna. The leaves of a fern unfurl. The petals of rose gentian, summer's arrival, pink on a yellow center, are delicate and dead on the pond shore. Dew drops from golden aster.

At the pond shore, the cardinal flower. At the pond shore, boneset, Joe Pye weed, goldenrod. In the fields, milkweed. In the fields, butterfly weed. Golden asters sunning themselves. The flat grass of deer beds. In the fields, goldenrod in bloom. Lupine petals dry on the forest floor. On the forest floor, partridge berry. On the forest floor, tea berry. In the dry sun, sweet fern. In the fields, switch grass.

At the fields' edges, the wolves. They give a chorus howl, rallying one another. The dinner death-dance has begun.

In early evening, the deer, too, are hungry. They have survived a whole day from predators. But still, there is the evening to live through. The light is low. A white-tailed deer turns her ears. A sound echoes through the trees, but in summer, the trees full and green with leaves, the sound of a musket shot is dampened. Barn owls, tawny owls, magpies, hawks, jackdaws, and snakes, all seeking food. Along the roadside, the wolf traps set out by the colonists, and the wolf pack running forward.

Alice Bradford

Up the hill we went, the pitchers swinging by our sides. At forty, I could see new ways I had lived my life ungodly. Not in big deeds—not murder, nor gluttony, nor sloth—but in the wish to never make another person feel ill-suited. In my hope for others' comfort, I missed something far greater: honesty. It was easier to speak about others, as Susanna did, or talk about the pragmatic qualities of our daily lives in Plymouth—the women's schedule of mending, washing, milking, cooking, feeding, gardening, mothering, as I did with Elizabeth, then to call one another toward something deeper.

Elizabeth and I had reached the water. We washed our hands. We filled up the pitchers. I appreciated the two of us quietly working together.

I liked Elizabeth, but I missed Dorothy. Wishing to bring her into the space betwixt us, I inquired of Elizabeth what she recalled of Dorothy.

Elizabeth peered at the ground, as if reading the grass for signs.

She didn't seem well, she said. *It became more pronounced the longer we were on the ship.*

I wanted to tell her of the sadness in Dorothy I witnessed, but there was no place to begin. I kept quiet.

There was a boy. Jasper. The youngest of the Mores.

I knew the children she spoke of, sent away by their father without their mother's knowledge, and given to us by Weston, along with a sum from their uncle. Their father wanted to rise in politics. Lord Zouche had said, *If you can't take care of your home, how do you expect the King to think you can take care of the country?* He needed to get rid of them to increase his standing.

By the year of our Lord sixteen hundred and thirty, Richard More was twelve, in William Brewster's care, and had recently fulfilled his indentured servitude. But as there was no parent or sibling to care for him, he still lived with Brewster as his servant.

Quieter than Richard, almost of a different stock. A sweet boy. She took to him. And when he perished she—did not take it well.

Elizabeth picked at her cuticle. I understood that this was all she would say. From those few words I would have to piece together all that they implied.

She asked my opinion of how the dinner went and what I thought of the new arrivals. I let the conversation shift.

How was Master Morton permitted back?

Further punishment, I imagine.

I didn't know. My husband was furious about it, but my role was to instill confidence.

We were turning back toward the colony when a shot rang out. A sound not from the colony, but beyond the fences, where we were. A close-by sound.

When I heard it I thought, *I do not want to die.*

A musket.

Indians, I thought. *An Indian attack.*

As fast as we could, we ran back toward whence we had come. Through the darkening footpath, our pitchers sloshing, to our husbands at the meetinghouse.

Newcomen

In the clearing, then through it, at the water.

Jim, a voice said.

John Newcomen turned his head. He saw the dull tip of a musket.

He'll kill me without knowing my name, Newcomen thought.

Jim, John Billington said. *Have another look.*

He'd come this far, across the Atlantic. Survived seven weeks at sea. Had not died from storm, pirates, the seamen's illness. Now, this man. For a single acre.

Newcomen closed his eyes.

The sunlight dappled through fluttering leaves, which he could see though his eyes were shut. He'd left Eugenia in her good summer dress, the wind blowing. Eugenia at the top of the hill, the smile she gave him in recognition. How he preferred to watch her when she did not know he was looking.

His mother's hand across his forehead, her worried expression when he had a fever. The time she took him to see the geese in their grand flight south.

Newcomen turned to Billington to try to say anything to pardon himself from this wild man's whims.

Then a deep inward plunge, the face of his stepfather, glassy-eyed with drink, pulling him from his bed, and under it, into a hole whose depths were boundless.

John Billington

Billington jabbed the barrel of the gun into the thin ligaments of Newcomen's neck.

Not a move, Billington said, and slid the gun barrel down the man's spine. He took two paces back.

There was a twitch of the neck, or a movement, or perhaps John Billington was seeing things. His eyes registered motion.

He pulled the trigger.

The shot echoed off trees and startled the birds. Three deer bounded toward the brook. The beavers dipped into the water, swam farther upstream, going against the current as fast as they could.

He'd done it, hadn't he, Billington? Under pressure, he was. The elders' curse against him had proven them right. A body of a newcomer, dead.

At the shot, he himself jumped. He knew his rifle, its work on deer and geese and even beavers, though the shot ruined the pelt. He knew his rifle but not the man before him, nor the weight of fifteen stones he would now have to drag across the forest to somewhere.

Was his name not Jim?

He could call for help. Say an Indian had done this or say he'd seen him fall. That would cause a fine stir in Governor William Bradford, now wouldn't it?

The forest was indifferent, as indifferent as it had been when Bradford ordered the men to drag the dying colonists' bodies out into the woods, prop them up against trees, and put muskets in their arms so that Plymouth appeared to have far more healthy colonists than it did.

Nature did not notice.

John Billington paced. Three birds flew out from a pine tree. He heard the rustling of a larger animal making haste away. Then the wind and just him, Billington, alone with a dead man, blood blooming through his tunic.

Aye, no one would say this was an accident. Certainly not Bradford, who had it out for him, ever since he'd refused to move on the *Mayflower* and give his space over. One must challenge men who think they are better than the rest. It all could be blamed on these wretched puritans, ruining courageous adventurers such as himself.

Billington lifted Newcomen's right leg. Heavy. Damn it, he'd done it. *Think, Billington.* Bradford won't want news of a murder. He'll have no choice but to pardon him, otherwise word would spread to England. Word of a murder would equal fewer colonists and therefore less money for Bradford.

Billington dragged the body of Newcomen by the arms. John Billington was fifty, newly aware of the limits of his body, and weaker than he thought he would ever be. Newcomen caught on a log and then on a root. His cloak caught, then his boot. It was no use. Billington let go of Newcomen's heft. His head was as floppy as a newborn's, but significantly heavier. It dropped against a fallen tree.

The day had been beautiful until he saw Newcomen. This place would have been bountiful if he were a free man. He should have been free seven years earlier, when the *Mayflower* went off course. Had the hypocrites been fair-minded, this would have never happened. The King's Charter was invalid. They weren't in Virginia, as the charter granted, so he should never have been an indentured man to them.

He would not say this man's death was an accident. He honored himself to never descend to lies, like the hypocrites and Captain Shrimp. No, he'd say he shot him. That's what he'd done and he would say it.

Billington picked up the body, again, and continued to drag him. But what would he do once he got to the palisade? Carry a dead man through it? Even if he wanted to, he was no longer strong enough.

Newcomen was not due the acre next to his field. That land was Billington's land. Standish had put him there to threaten Billington. He'd given another man his land to provoke. Standish thought he was above the law he set. He did whatever he pleased because he was the Captain.

Billington propped the body against his oak tree and walked toward his house.

At the palisade, he tipped his hat to the guard, a Miller boy. It would not be long before that Miller boy would be coming for him.

When Billington arrived at the gate of his house, he called to his wife.

Eleanor yelled back from inside, *What ye want!*

How soon their lives would change. He hesitated.

The goats brayed. Inside the fence, a young goat cried and cried and cried.

Billington looked out to see the goat's mother, hurtling herself down the hill toward them.

She's coming, he whispered.

The female goat propelled herself forward across the colony with the reckless speed of a new mother. She pushed the gate open with her long nose, and placed her body and her udders near the infant. The baby goat banged his head against his mother's udder, until he found her teat, and gulped for milk.

Billington's wife stepped onto the threshold.

What did ye do? she said.

She had her hands on her hips and blew the curl that fell into her face, a gesture he loved. Oh, how he hated what he would have to tell her.

Alice Bradford

It was God's blessing that we were not followed, nor were caught, as I thought it then. When we reached the meetinghouse, the dinner was nearing its decline. Bones and crusts littered the plates. Men and women were loud, leaning into one another—loosened by beer and wine. I saw the room differently upon my return. Teeth gnashed. A dozen seamen were playing cards. One had his head down on the table, already drunk. Candles cried their wax tears.

We often do not know what things mean to us until they are broken.

No one, it seemed, had heard the gunshot. I went swiftly to my husband and relayed the news in a loud whisper.

Where is Joseph? I asked him.

Right here, he said, and extended his hand beneath the table. But under the table were only muddy boots on hairy legs.

Where? I asked, no longer quiet or patient or calm or a governor's wife. Only a mother.

I pushed betwixt the men's chairs, betwixt the men's legs.

Hello there, Thomas Weston said.

Susanna touched my elbow.

Good Wife, she said, and urged me to her table.

There, in the braided basket, was Joseph, asleep. The fear had made me think all would fall away, that I would lose everything in this earthly world and I newly understood how much I cared for the earthly, how much I wanted more than what God intended, if what He intended involved the death of those I loved.

There was a rumbling as Standish started for the exit. The party pressed forward to the doors of the meeting-house, to see what was the commotion.

Come in, come in, Myles Standish called, standing at the door, ushering forward three servants who had been running toward him. They said they had heard gunfire. Captain Standish had his gun ready and it was the only time I had been thankful to see it.

Just kill it, I thought. *Just kill it and don't get killed yourself*, I urged Standish, in my thoughts.

Myles Standish gathered the militia, every able-bodied man in the colony, each of whom took a musket that was leaning against the far wall of the meetinghouse. My husband stepped forward. So did John.

No, I said, for Dorothy as much as for myself, holding on to both of their arms. But William and John both broke free of me.

John picked up the gun. I could see this was his first time holding a weapon such as this and I could see how much he wished to be a pleasing son to his father. And out the doors they went, to defend us, to see what was causing God's displeasure.

Eleanor Billington

Good Wife! my husband called from the yard, in a tone too serious to be a welcoming sign.

What trouble do I have to get ye out of now, Good Husband?

I knew this was not going to be pleasant, but I wasn't ready to give up our way. I thought my humor might help.

I'm afraid you won't be able to help this time.

He appeared in the doorway, blood on his cheek.

What's all this? I asked.

That newcomer.

I watched him. He'd gone and finally done what I feared he always might.

Where is he? I said.

I made a start to bolt out into the colony, and beyond it into the fields. He held up his hand, the world's sign for stop, as if urging me and the world to halt. He had done the irrevocable.

He's dead, Eleanor.

What did he do?

Took down my tree.

I raised my eyebrows.

I warned him.

I pursed my lips.

Ah, hell. Newcomen wasn't the problem. It wasn't right, but I've gone and done it.

I thought for a minute.

Your musket misfired.

It didn't.

They won't—I couldn't say it. *They'll pardon you. Bradford won't want blood on his hands.*

Hard to market a colony with murderers.

You aren't a murderer, John. It was a crime of passion, say. Your humors were temporarily unbalanced. The drink.

He just looked at the dirt.

No one knows it was you.

I can't leave him there. It's not right for a man to be left like that.

I tried to persuade him, I did, to pretend as if it never happened. But gentleman that he was, he would not leave that body.

We walked fast—but slowed our pace as we passed the meetinghouse—to where he'd laid Newcomen near the oak tree, his head resting on a fallen log.

I heard a guttural sound, and we both inched closer to Newcomen. The man lurched upright, opened his mouth wide, and gasped.

He lives! I said.

But no sooner had I said it then he slammed back down on the log.

My husband just stood there shaking his head.

Say it was an accident. It's Standish's fault, leaving us to fend for ourselves while he enjoys the fat of a roasted duck.

No, he said. *I've done it, Eleanor. I'm not a man to lie about what I've done. I have to accept my fate. Hanging, no doubt.*

I turned away from him. I stared at the vacant field that had never bothered me. Now it did. I almost said *John the younger*, almost told him to speak of our son's death as why he did what he did. But I did not. I took the sleeve of my dress and wiped away the blood on my husband's face. The mark of a stranger's blood smeared on my newly washed dress. It didn't matter.

We heard a crowd rumbling.

Here come the Savages, I said.

A dozen hypocrites and a handful of fight-eager, drunken seamen—guns raised, some still with stew-smattered napkins on their shoulders, a few in the back carrying their cups—yelled *Huzzah!* and charged toward us.

Newcomen's body lay there, his dead eyes wide open. I went to him and with my fingers shut his lids.

Standish charged my way, his rifle high, the men behind him, with Edward Winslow in the back next to that coward who sends everyone else to do his work, Governor Bradford.

Ten paces from the body, they stopped short.

I steadied a smile.

Gentlemen, I said, and gave a curtsy, my best curtsy.

I stood above Newcomen.

My husband was behind the tree, slender enough to not be seen. Only a few more minutes of freedom. I understood why he lingered there. That night I'd learn—but it shan't have been surprising—that his parting gift to me was drinking all the liquor Morton had given us.

Standish took one look at Newcomen, one look at me, and yelled, *Billington!*

What have ye done? said Bradford, running forward.

The militia boys, those paid hands, those traitors, called, *Murder!*

Not even knowing what had happened.

The blood was through Newcomen's tunic and his cloak.

My husband stepped from behind the tree, slowly, like a bear awoken at the end of winter. You would not know he was afraid, unless you saw his thumb tapping against his left leg. As a boy . . . Why speak it? No one cares of us.

I'll tell it anyway. As a boy, he watched his mother have her head chopped off with a dull blade in the town square, when he was not even tall enough to reach the barstool. It took ten chops, he said. The crowd laughed at her, called, *Again, again.* The blood splattered on his face. That's how close he stayed to her.

She'd have died soon anyway. Her body was covered with white paint to make herself look paler, as was the fashion, but also to disguise the sores on her arms. The great pox, syphilis. Sad, common women like me dying that way in London, my own mother dying that way before the law could get her. One of the bishop's hens of Winchester.

Standish picked up Newcomen's arm. Dead.

He said, *What did ye do?*

I looked at my husband, willing him to say it was an accident. His word against a dead man's.

You sold him land that was mine.

That man never listened to me when he needed to.

Arrest him, Bradford said to Standish.

Standish motioned to Hopkins and Samuel, two newly freed servants. Barely men. The age John the younger would have been.

They took my husband by the arms.

A seaman hoisted Newcomen over his shoulder. Once they got near the meetinghouse, Bradford and Winslow took the body, to appear as if they had carried it all along.

I followed alongside. I yelled what Standish needed to hear, *You think him guilty before you know the story*, though he dothn't have ears, hearing only what he wanted to.

I've been calling the dead man Newcomen, but there's something else.

What is this man's name? Bradford asked.

And no one knew.

Alice Bradford

The new colonists pressed forward.

Outside the meetinghouse, Captain Standish walked closely behind Master Billington. His wife, Eleanor, ran beside Standish, calling obscenities. At the back of the procession, my husband and Susanna's husband carried the dead body of the man who looked like Johannes. John was his name, and his surname I never knew, so here I have called him Newcomen.

Inside the meetinghouse, women set down their drinks, picked up their children, moved toward the windows and thresholds, spread out onto the dirt, and watched. Pregnant women held on tightly to their stomachs, afraid of what feeling alarmed could do to their growing infants.

This was not the welcome we wanted for the newcomers.

Let go of me! Billington cried.

For reasons I still do not understand, Captain Standish loosened his hold.

John Billington yanked his own arm back.

What say ye, Master Billington? my husband asked.

You gave my very land away.

What say ye of this man, shot dead?

You gave my land away, provoked me, disrespected me. I who have outlasted fifty, outlasted a hundred of you hypocrites, with God's good grace.

The parishioners gasped.

Where is God's just hand, you hypocrites? I ask ye thus! And now, provoked, given no choice, you poked me like a bear in the pits. On a chain I was and like the hungry dogs you are, you made me do this.

So you confess? asked Standish.

Billington shook his head like a man just released from the drunk tank.

Did you shoot this man? asked William.

My husband and Susanna's husband had set the body down. The flies were circling around John Newcomen's head. One landed on his bluing lips. It is not right to care for the dead this way. I hoped this argument would end soon and we could give this stranger a proper burial.

If word gets out you have a murderer in this colony, how will that be for your profit, Governor Bradford?

My husband stepped closer to Billington. So close his spittle could flash across Billington's face.

What if, Governor Bradford, word gets out that a settler has been killed, and another settler murdered? How many new settlers would that yield you, Governor Bradford? You will not kill me.

This is the first and it will be the last. We will not tolerate murderers.

A voice in the crowd said, *It isn't the first.*

Eleanor Billington stepped forward.

What of your own wife? she said sweetly.

Within me was a scream. A scream that had waited a decade to escape. All the newcomers turned.

William did not charge as I thought he might. Instead, he clenched his jaw and turned toward her husband.

Did you, or did you not, kill this man?

Billington did not speak for a very long few moments. And when he did, when my husband held his stare and his scorn, Billington said, *I've said all I will say.*

Take him away, Bradford called to Captain Standish, who motioned for two indentured servants. Each took one arm and led Billington to the room beneath the meetinghouse.

Joseph cried, his bottom was wet, and I was thankful for the excuse to go home. I called for Mercy and William the younger to come with me and outstretched my hand. I wanted to hold everything I loved. They both ran over.

I'm a bear, Mercy said, growling, *and bears do not live in houses.* Even as a child she chose to be too close to danger. William the younger stood by me.

One must outwardly and inwardly be what one is. The only sumptuary law we had was of disguises. I would again teach Mercy about the importance of being what one was.

You are a girl, Mercy, who fears God. It is time to go home and change your brother.

Children are born chosen by God—or not—but still, they must be taught.

Susanna lumbered over to me and we hooked arms. She was not herself, as one would expect. When pregnant, one did not stare at the moon, so the children would not be sleepwalkers or lunatics. Women crossed no paths with rabbits, so their children would not grow a harelip. And if a pregnant woman was startled it could cause the child to grow a sixth finger.

She told me she had been scared and had not felt the baby since.

The child will be healthy, you'll see. Let's get you home.

But one never knew what it would please God to do.

Eleanor Billington

S o my husband had changed his mind about confession. He did not say he did it. That was one of the wiser things he had done in his lifetime. There was a chance.

I came home to the goats and our son, Francis, sleeping by the fireplace. I went for the shelf where we kept the wine, intending to split it with Francis, the first offering to our son of our good liquor, when he'd lived before on watery beer. I opened the bottle and tilted it. There was nary a drop.

I looked for the flask. Gone. Getting himself killed and drinking all our liquor.

Sure, they had not said yet what his punishment would be, but I knew. We all did. This was Standish's chance. This was Bradford's opportunity to kill the truth forever. Punishing my husband for shooting a man on his own property, who would not leave, was a disguise for what they really wanted to punish him for: speaking out against them.

How could I get my husband out of this? I needed to think, which was harder to do without an evening drink and without dinner. He'd returned with a dead man instead of a deer. There was pie, but I hadn't an appetite for it.

I took a walk. Out into the field, crying despite myself, angry at everything. Sassafras scratching against my arms, which I hated, hooting owls high in the trees, which I despised, and the distant howl of wolves.

There was no one left to help me fight against them, except Francis.

I walked for an hour, maybe longer, until I knew not the way.

Go home, a voice said unto me.

I felt the prickling of my skin, the kind that comes when someone says something true, too true, and unexpected.

Go home and care for your son.

A breeze came from behind and pushed me toward the home my husband and I had built. Approaching it again, by full moon's light, I saw it with the eyes of one who could lose everything. I'd split the wood for the beams. He'd hammered and hoisted and roofed it. Our eldest son was buried behind back. I did not wish to be far away from him, to be banished and to never return to my boy. I could not leave him and I could not leave this. This was my home.

Our land was here, our house was here, our son was here. They'd give me nothing for it, pence, I'm sure, and where else could I go? Not back to London, where I had nothing and no longer knew a soul. Tom Morton could be a help. He had written about my husband as a fine man, a greater man than the people who ran Plymouth. *Beloved by many*, he called my husband.

But Morton was a jolly old drunkard and had enough money to do what he pleased. He had no understanding of the daily needs of us commoners. He was a man for celebrations. And he was charged himself, and liable to be the next murdered the first chance they could blame something on him. A passage back to London would cost me the value of this land and house. I was stuck here, you see.

I climbed into bed and thought of how this was the first time I'd slept in a bed without John since the eve of our wedding day, twenty-five years before. Francis joined me. I watched my young son sleeping so close next to me, lightly snoring. The mother and baby goat leapt in, too, their barnyard smells something soothing. Our bodies pressed together, warming the cool evening air.

Yes, I resolved, or yes, I was resigned to it. Here I would stay and here I would watch the colony kill my husband.

Alice Bradford

T hat night, Billington was committed to the fort. John shared William the younger's bed, and William, sweet boy, offered his blanket, eager as he was to have an older brother.

In haste, my husband wrote to John Winthrop, the new Massachusetts Bay Colony governor, seeking his advice. But he was not seeking his advice, exactly, as much as he was confirming his good favor with the King by including the King's favorite into his decision. What, he asked Winthrop, would be a firm discipline but not lose him favor with the colonists? He wanted to send the message that Plymouth was not a colony to come to if you were a criminal.

And how to do this without news getting to London and rumors spreading that Plymouth was unsafe? William would have liked—we all would have then—to see

Billington dead. He also told Governor Winthrop that the outlawed Morton had arrived on the *Gifte*.

I trust you'll know what to do with him, William wrote.

Our house was full. Quietly, my husband complained that the food we needed to feed all the newcomers would cause our own daily supply to be cut in half. There was also Thomas Morton to reckon with. William asked the price Morton had paid for the passage, and what portion of the fee the colony would receive. Weston said the accountant applied it to our debt, but he would have to check with him upon return to London. My husband was distraught by this, at the costs of it all, and the timing of Billington's murder.

But now, at least, we will be done with him, I said.

I lit a candle to do a bit more needlework—my hands needed to be kept busy—and William looked at me askance.

That did not stop the wick from burning so he said, *Good Wife, why must you cost us so?*

I put out the candle and reached for him. I wanted to press together all that I had and all that I loved and all, I knew, I would one day lose.

He touched me, betwixt my legs, and looked at me with fondness. His intention was not, as I had thought, to chastise me. A look from him that only I knew. And Dorothy. The cool air and our warm bodies.

This was not the time for God's earthly blessing—the room was too full this evening—but I thought of other days. Always at the brink I held my breath.

Once he was nearly there, he would give a small gasp—a favorite sound—but also, too, from there he was no longer mine. His body would urge him onward, his muscles would tense, his flat palm would seem as if it could push through the wall. I would squeeze him closer into me. It was always him I was after.

I put my finger to my body, discreetly, and circled there. Him hard and deep inside me, his stubble rough against my chin, him bent down in prayer to my body, no sweat, not him, rarely sweat, and in that wave and crest I felt the ocean rise and then slowly, slowly creep away.

In the morning, the men buried John Newcomen in the soft dirt atop Burial Hill. No one knew him enough to speak of him, but we said we hoped it pleased God to bid him rest.

We'll have a trial, my husband said that afternoon. My husband and Susanna's husband culled the names of the twelve most honest men in the colony to serve as jurors.

John Billington stayed a week beneath the meeting-house.

On the morning of the trial, I woke to the sound of wolves howling at the edges of the colony. I'd seen a pack kill one of its own once. At sunset, in the clearing, I had gone to the brook. The rushing water disguised all sounds around it. When my pitchers were full I started back home. I saw it. A wolf lying on the ground, still lifting its head to bite back, its body in bloody tufts, some innards beginning their decline outward through a lesion in the stomach. Three wolves around it, barking, baring teeth, biting and tearing. The weakest killed: That was nature. Divine providence was everywhere present.

My husband and I held hands to the meetinghouse. Little William ran up alongside us, said, *Three hands*, and broke the chain betwixt us. I turned for John, sensing his eyes on my back, and urged him to join us. John gave the smile of one unaccustomed to such inclusion, then shook his head no, as if to remind me he was no longer a boy, and too old for such shows of affection. We outgrow it, don't we, the expression of that fierce edge that is always a part of love?

Eleanor Billington

T he news of my husband's trial spread out of Plymouth, north to Boston and Salem, through the trading posts and towns in between. The law said twelve honest men would be chosen as jurors. The law said a *fair trial*, and instead Bradford chose hypocrite jurors who hated us to decide the fate of my husband.

Bradford chose twelve he called *the most honest men*, but they were just his friends, all of whom hated my husband as much as Bradford. There was nothing fair or honest about the trial of my husband, just as there had been nothing fair about how these hypocrites regarded us since the beginning. William Bradford did not want honesty. He wanted collusion. He wanted us to go along, just go along, his flock of sheep, and never speak the truth of our ill treatment.

At my husband's trial, the meetinghouse was full, perhaps even fuller than at Pastor Lyford's trial. The hypocrite women fanned themselves. Men set down their guns and rolled up their sleeves. Everyone's eyes were on my husband, then the people glanced back at me. I caught their stares and held my chin high.

And what happened, Master Billington? Captain Shrimp asked him.

It was in defense.

And what were ye defending? Captain Shrimp asked, incredulity in his voice.

They would have called the deer to the witness stand, if they could, before believing my husband's good word.

Billington land, my husband said.

I put my head in my hands. That Good Husband could have at least tried to lie to save himself.

The trial took a break for the jury to deliberate.

When Pastor Lyford was found guilty he had six months to arrange his exit. I knew they'd never be so kind to my husband, no matter how many tears he shed. He was not of wealth or clergy. But my husband shan't shed tears, because he was not an actor nor a pastor, but a man of truth.

Not even an hour had passed. All hearsay. No one was alive who saw what happened, save my husband. And he was being tried for killing a man so valuable to the colonists they did not even know his surname.

And how do thee find Master Billington? Bradford asked the jury.

Guilty, Edward Winslow said, and that self-righteous crowd cheered.

My husband lowered his head.

Don't do that, I thought. He had to look out at them, like an honest man, never stoop or bow to them.

Might I go home to gather my things? my husband asked Bradford.

Myles Standish answered for Bradford.

What things, Master Billington, will you possibly need at the gallows?

The crowd laughed.

Take him away, Bradford said, and the crowd cheered.

I looked at those who had benefited from my husband. My husband had said and done what they wished to. The former indentured servants were not cheering, bless them, but they were not arguing against the rest, either. They admired my husband but they wouldn't speak out here, for him, in public. They would not risk their lives. Cowards.

There was one exception. A young man, holding an infant girl, chubby and pink, looked to his neighbors and said, *Stop!* His one voice was not enough to do anything against the ocean of the crowd, but I heard it.

I pushed my way forward and held tight to Francis's hand as I did. He was approaching manhood himself, but I held on to him as if he were still the younger boy I imagined him to be. I reached my husband, touched his weak arm, squeezed.

I love ye, I said. *I will always love ye.*

Myles Standish pushed my husband forward, and away from me.

It was lunchtime on Friday and the hanging was sched-
uled for the following Wednesday. Just enough time, I
knew, to properly advertise the execution to the neighboring towns. Anything to get more of a profit.

I knew what I had to do, my last chance. I must go to
Mistress Bradford. My husband, failing to convince toads,
had wrecked his chances by blaming those with power.
Those hypocrites hate most any criticism that gives them
embarrassment. I had to get to Alice, alone, and plead his
case.

Alice Bradford

I had slept little the night before Billington's trial. After the trial, I lay down with Joseph. Mercy was with Susanna. I could hear the children's high-pitched laughs. William the younger was working with his father.

But no sooner had I closed my eyes when at my door there was a knocking. The warming air sauntered in and along with it, Eleanor Billington. Previously, I had conversations with her only when passing through the colony—to the brook with buckets, while milking the cows—and the one time I went to her house to speak with her about her husband. Never at my door. Never so forwardly had she addressed me, the governor's wife.

She carried a loaf of bread in one hand and yelled back to her son and two goats to stay put in the garden. Where would they go? It was a command she said in habit, I imagine, when one assumes their child will cause trouble.

I came to see that threat we feared was not the Wampanoag—our treaty with Massasoit had been long-standing—nor the unknowns beyond the colony's fences. Instead, the threat came from within our own community. Her husband would have his punishment in five days. The sight of her stirred fear in me.

What did Eleanor Billington wish to speak to me about? From the anger directed at her son, and the bread in her hand, I sensed that she was nervous. Did the bread indicate she wanted something? I could not pardon her husband.

Tea? I asked.

Eleanor nodded.

The teapot was Dorothy's, after it was her grand-mother's, with one fine, hair-thin crack, a white teapot with red English roses. I filled it with hot water, set it down. Such a long time it seemed to take for the tea to steep.

Eleanor took little time to tell me her request. She wanted a pardon for her husband. She said it was a momentary imbalance of bodily humors.

I thought, but did not say, *The momentary lapse has lasted ten years.*

I feigned thinking on it. I apologized to her for her husband's outcome.

It was not a fair trial, she said. *Every juror was one of you. None of us.*

I raised my eyebrows. She was not practiced in niceties, had no training at persuasion, only force.

Our son, she said.

That was it. The thing I had nearly forgotten, so ungodly I was. But also, God has his methods.

My husband wasn't thinking right, she said.

My house was dark. The windows were covered to keep out the insects, particularly mosquitos and horse flies, and to keep the air pleasing. The humming of the insects was the only thing I ordinarily hated in summer.

We are a body politic, I said, reminding her of our original compact. *We are one in the same*, I said. *There cannot be murderers in our colony. Surely you understand.*

Her face went grave and she looked down. When she looked up again, she was wearing a smile. What I said had given her insult.

If he were not your husband—but I stopped short of saying more.

Eleanor wore a look similar to the one I had in my childish years, when the sermons were boring to me. I sat in church pews and practiced the appropriate way to look enrapt, and after church, the way to speak to mothers and cousins when telling them I was sorry for their losses.

I heard Mercy cry from outside, but more than hear, I felt the tether betwixt us. I should have rejoiced if God chose her to be spared from the grief of this world. And yet there was great difficulty in reconciling what I should feel with what I did feel. I said then and there to God, *Prithee keep her safe and let her life be a long and prosperous one.* That prayer, in vain, went unfulfilled.

Eleanor complimented the teacups. So perhaps she did know some manners after all.

I thanked her and said they were Dorothy's.

The one who jumped off the ship?

She slipped, I corrected, sending her a certain missive I did not myself fully believe. I set down my tea too quickly on the saucer and it rattled. I tried to muffle the sound by covering the cup. My hands where Dorothy's had been, and her mother's, and her grandmother's.

Self-murder, Eleanor said. *Not a thing your husband would wish to speak of.*

It was then that something occurred to me. With William's standing, Dorothy's self-murder would not only be scandalous, but it would be cause to give her possessions to the King. A person who self-murdered had committed a grievous crime against the state and, like all criminals, had fines to pay. The family of a self-murderer owed their belongings to the King in penalty. No matter, of course, of God's view, who tells us it is the worst of sins.

I suddenly knew I must get Eleanor out of my house, for I was not well. *One mustn't cry*, I repeated to myself.

I'm sorry I cannot help you, I said, and stood from the table.

Eleanor took a gulp of tea and started for the door. But she stopped. She turned to me. Over her shoulder, I saw the heavy door begin to creak open on its own accord. By wind or by spirit, I could not say.

She opened her mouth, then closed it.

You've never loved or understood anything, she said. *He married you because you are simple.*

I knew I was a governor's wife then, for I smiled placidly at her and wished her well.

She walked out. Surprisingly, she closed the gate gently in her exit.

Eleanor Billington

If I am going to my grave, I'm going to it honestly. The Billington way. Take down a peg those who think they are better than us.

They left my husband beneath the meetinghouse and fed him only the fallen, fly-munched ears of corn, which everyone knows kills the calves.

He's thirsty, I said to Standish, whenever I found him milling about.

He's hungry and needs meat, I'd say.

Why? Standish asked. *To keep him alive longer? He's chosen the rope, mistress. Day's cold corn will not kill him. His own temperament did that.*

No respect for the living or the dead.

So I spoke it aloud. All of it. Right after the dinner bell. As the newcomers and colonists made their way to the meetinghouse, I stood at the top of the hill. I waited for the crowd. When there was enough of them, I spoke.

Hear, ye! My husband was not the first murderer of this colony! That was him!

I pointed through the people, straight to Governor Bradford.

And him! I pointed at the Shrimp.

I said what should have been my husband's final words to William Bradford.

I wish to speak of Dorothy Bradford.

The crowd was rapt, staring at me. It wasn't that I cared about Dorothy. If Bradford were to bring shame on my family, I would bring shame on him.

Governor Bradford charged forward, no longer a false smile across his face.

He was before me, yelling, *Stop!*

He had me pinned. The crowd was behind me and he was before.

Francis stepped betwixt us.

William Bradford stared at me. I was what he wanted to remove from the world. But he could not. He could not remove differing opinion. He could not remove truth.

Let them stare, thought I. I would not scare.

I said more and more, rising in spirit and wrath as I spoke until Myles Standish pushed me into the meetinghouse.

Alice Bradford

I was on my way to the field when I saw Myles Standish pull Eleanor by her right arm.

She turned, yelling, *All you righteous righteous righteous.*

She looked at me and spit on the ground.

Captain Standish led her toward the meetinghouse. She only had so far that her voice would carry to my ears, and the ears of the men and woman stepping down from ladders, out of their gardens, closing the gate, walking toward the commotion. Soon she would be in the room adjoining her husband, beneath the meetinghouse.

No one will say it. God's plan, you all say.

She had the audience she wanted. Twenty people were turned, watching her, more were stepping away from their labor and toward her spectacle.

Her son, fifteen, grabbed hold of her arm and spoke something to her. She yanked her arm away.

Get out of here, I imagined her saying.

Let her speak, someone behind me said. It was Richard More, the only surviving More child. He had been recently released from servitude. As a man of no power, he needed my husband's good favor.

I wish to speak of Dorothy Bradford. Ask him of his first wife, Eleanor said, pointing to my husband. *His very own wife. Ask him what happened to her.*

Myles Standish opened the door to the meetinghouse. He tried to cross the threshold but Eleanor gripped the frame.

You think my husband was the first murderer. But I'll tell thee. His—at this she pointed to my husband—*first wife, offed herself. Took one look at what he'd dragged her to*—

Enough! William yelled.

I could see he was shaking.

—*and jumped off the ship.*

Back and forth she was swaying, as Standish tried to push her into the meetinghouse. She gripped the doorframe and pulled herself back out.

Dorothy Bradford was the first who died of unnatural causes. Driven to self-murder by her own husband's cruelty, Eleanor said. *No patience, had he, for her grief!*

Did the crowd gasp? It felt as if they did.

There are things we do that cannot be taken back. Things that, once done, are irrevocable. This was Eleanor's.

She was clawing her way from Standish's grip. She was over the edge now, out of the threshold, but where would she go?

Enough! My husband repeated.

The crowd was parting for him. They turned toward his voice, wondering what would unfold. William walked in quick strides, no longer the ploughman but the governor. At once he was before her.

Eleanor called, *Save yourselves! Get back on that ship before the Master departs!*

She got that much out before William shoved her shoulders and back she went through the doorframe.

I heard a crack, so piercing, I imagined it to be her arm that snapped in two.

Eleanor Billington let out a yelp.

Hang her! some of the elders called.

The newcomers, watching.

Could the crowd whirl even the new arrivals up into the chaos?

Don't leave, I thought. *And prithee do not think of us this way.*

With Eleanor inside, the crowd became chattery, made talkative by the excitement of Eleanor's speech.

I walked back to our houses with Elizabeth and Susanna. I thought of all there was left to do before the execution, to prepare for the visitors from neighboring towns. Bread to bake and stew to simmer. Straw beds to build, blankets to gather, and floor space to find. Likely, they would stay at the meetinghouse, just a floor betwixt them and the accused. The men still needed to build the gallows. Hopefully the visitors would make a few purchases, too.

Governor Winthrop had sent his regrets. I was thankful he would not be coming, for it meant less of a burden for us to be formal in our arrangements.

I thought of Dorothy. Her son was with the men now, nearly a man himself. He seemed to have grown into a polite boy, thus far. He took the plates and washed them on his own accord. He listened to his father with deference. He did not seem to dislike me. *Oh, Dorothy, if you could see him. Perhaps you can, though, every day, as your gaze falls downward upon us.*

Dorothy

O nce, crossing the bridge on the way to the market, as girls, we passed a man. In his eyes was a look that no longer submits. Alice glanced at me as if to say, *What will happen?* But I kept my eyes onward.

The man in the stand beside ours, the one who would later make coins disappear and re-emerge for my John, said, *Girls. A man has jumped.*

The vendors were leaving their eggs and vegetables, were surging toward the canal to see the spectacle. We were no different. I carried Prince, the black fowl I told my father was just, for some reason, not selling.

Along the canal, we pressed forward. A body lulled back and forth with the water. Dead. A man pulled him out. From the crowd, a woman screamed and ran forward.

In England, self-murder was a crime punished by God and the King. In England his wife would owe the King his possessions. But in Holland, his debts were absolved. In

Holland, a man had dominion over his body. In Holland, a wife could grieve. Long after, I thought of the woman running forward.

Why think of this? William would say, and turn back to his work. He would go back to the loom, go back to the fire, blow gently on the little flame. His interest was in perseverance. He looked to how God deemed us favorable and turned away from that which did not fit. Sadness only entered if it showed how God tested, but how He prevailed us.

Alice and I made up stories about the man we had seen earlier that morning. He'd gambled his week's wages and, stepping out on the walk home, sobered by the sunrise and reconsidering what he had just done, and who would not be fed because of it—his growing son, his patient wife, his young daughter—he concluded the world would be better off without him. He crossed the bridge to take himself home, stepped instead to the side, and after we passed and went forward to the market, he, perhaps considering his decision to be the best thing he had ever done for anyone else, his least selfish act, jumped.

Who wants to join a colony where the governor's wife was so inconsolable she committed self-murder? Instead, one wants to join a community founded on freedom. A place in God's honor. Where beaver is so plentiful, one cannot catch and skin them all. Where, as William wrote, *The schools of fish will never leave one hungry.*

Eleanor Billington

On the last day of September, in the year of our Lord sixteen hundred and thirty, the colonists gathered to watch. The righteous women were there, of course, gawking like the rest, then pretending to hide their faces in their husband's shoulders as if the death they supported was too much to bear.

Two grey dogs whimpered, then ran away rather than come to their puritan masters. They knew what these men were made of. Dogs are not fooled by fine cloth and endless quotations from Scripture.

I saw Francis Eaton, the town carpenter, who I'd known to be a profiteer since the *Mayflower*, when he'd benefited from selling his goat's milk at a high price to the thirsty on the ship. Here, he sold roasted chestnuts for the occasion of my husband's murder. Men would get full while my husband was killed.

People from the Massachusetts Bay Colony took the Wampanoag footpath south, a days-long journey, to watch the first hanging of a colonist in Plymouth. Plymouth, a land in God's good favor, showing signs of being touched by the ungodly. If it were not my own husband at the gallows, I would have enjoyed watching it myself.

Thomas Morton stood by me, good gentleman.

At eleven my husband emerged from the meeting-house, the minister beside him, my husband's head down as if bowing. His body slumped like the farmer he was, though I'd never noticed that about him before, the effect of all those years of bending. I wondered then how often I'd not stopped to really look at him.

People jammed through the meetinghouse doors to see him. More full than any service. Every person wants to feel that they have avoided death. For a few days longer, anyway.

Bodies lined up, blocking the windows.

Captain Shrimp started things off by saying my husband was guilty of murder and that he'd been given a fair trial.

Liar! I yelled.

Thomas Morton took my hand.

The crowd turned, most of it, but Shrimp was accustomed to talking loudly over any words a woman like me spoketh. He did not pause. A minister I did not recognize—from Marshfield, someone said—wore a sanctimonious expression. He was young. This would be the first sermon he would have five hundred listeners for.

In the minister's hand, I saw, was a primer book for priests. *The Convict's Visitor*. He opened the book. His voice was dry and his hand shook.

He did not begin with grace, instead he started with a stilted fury: *Master Billington, God has shut you up in a place of darkness. A violent death is soon to remove you from the land of the living.*

The crowd leaned and pressed foward, enraptured by the fate that was not theirs. This stranger extolled the lack of virtues in my husband.

He said, *Let us learn from what we now behold.*

The minister turned the book to my husband and put his finger there. There were parts for my husband. My husband's line: *O Lord, turn them from darkness to light.* He said it, he did, for my husband wanted to show them all he could read.

But no more, I said inwardly to him, *do not follow the lines of this minister.*

Now you say, the minister intonated with this finger.

My husband scanned it—I saw his eyes moving across the page—but he did not speaketh.

The minister registered this refusal and changed directions.

The minister said, *Consider, Master Billington, that now you must die before your time. Consider that there is a second possibility, for you to escape the second death. Though your sin be great, God can pardon it. Yea and He hath—upon deep and unfeigned repentance—forgiven those that have committed this sin which you are now to suffer for.*

My husband looked out into the crowd.

All the crowd saw was a criminal.

The minister said, *There are some in heaven who were once bloody sinners. Consider David . . .*

He went on about David.

The minister said, *God is a great forgiver, God is a great forgiver! So I say to you in His Name, the Lord is a great Forgiver. It is His name that can forgive transgression and sin. Consider presently it will be too late for you to think of these things when once you are dead.*

The minister spoke to the crowd, for this whole display was not for my husband, but intended to gain the minister more parishioners. He said, *Oh, consider it and let it break your hearts.*

My husband was both a criminal who should die and a sinner who deserved pity for how he refused to repent.

The minister called for all sinners among the crowd to repent. He looked out expectantly, as if a sinner would then step forward. But with the gallows so close, no one would, particularly the criminal.

The minister put his arm on my husband's shoulder, and said, *Let us pray.*

I expected my husband to protest, but he did not. He bowed his head.

Again he was told to confess his sins. *Oh, John Billington, repent of your wickidness!*

It was my gun, but it was not my volition. These hypocrites, that lying Shrimp—

Quiet, the minister said low and mean. I saw a glimpse of the man this minister boy would become. Thick brown hair over his eyes, fervent and never questioning himself. That kind of child, the most indignant and self-righteous, brought up to be that way from their fathers.

My husband added, *The investors promising bloom and delivering rot.*

Quiet. Quiet. God does not—

But even Shrimp was tired of the minister. He stepped forward and said, *Enough.*

My husband's last words?

I love thee, my son. I love thee, Eleanor.

Death near turned him a milk sop.

True, he was.

A true, true fool.

Standish led my husband out of the meetinghouse, to the gallows erected by the sons of the hypocrites, including William Bradford's son John.

Standish guided my husband up the stairs. The last moment drew near. He pulled the cap over his eyes. It happened fast and slow at once. When in the presence of a life ending, one thinks the world should shudder, too, but it does not. Standish kicked the crate John's feet stood upon. My husband launched down into eternity. John's body shook, then stopped. The crowd cheered.

He hung there half an hour before he was permitted to be cut down.

❁

Francis Eaton made quite the profit. And so, too, did Bradford and the rest of the hypocrites. All those people coming into town, purchasing oxen they'd walk back to Boston, buying food and ale to watch my husband hang. But little did I know there was another impending conviction. Two officials from Salem waited until the crowd dispersed to take each of Tom Morton's arms.

I turned, ready to fight myself.

What is this? Tom asked, gentlemanly, but these men were not gentlemen, they were looking for more death.

You are wanted, Thomas Morton, for slander and speaking out against the King.

Let him go, I yelled. I'd had enough.

One of the men pushed me down in the dirt. Bloodied my lip, he did. Of course they took him anyway.

It was his *New Canaan*, his version of life in the colony, the true depiction of the hypocrites, catching up to him. Tom was not even given a trial, but ordered to be banished from Plymouth and the Massachusetts Bay Colony, and sent, once again, back to England.

The man with the infant daughter came to me.

Your husband saved my girl, he said.

What's this?

I had not known anything about John saving a girl.

Found a priest to baptize her, he did, and now look at her.

Before me was a dough-cheeked baby, healthy as can be. My husband had said nothing to me of this. But that was his way. He didn't boast of what he did for others.

If there is anything I can do, the father said.

I thanked him. At least someone had noticed.

On the walk home, I heard the profit jingling in Eaton's pocket. I resolved to get my son out of here as fast as I could.

Two servants returned my husband to me that afternoon. He was buried beneath the oldest oak tree. I go there and sit on Sundays, watch the birds, call him Good Husband and remind him of all the ways he should be thankful for me.

Now it's just me and Francis. They took our land. Said I was not fit to care for it. What John, John the younger, Francis, and I had labored on these past ten years.

In those weeks after, I thought our friends would come and check on me, but few did. They stayed away, as if my husband's murder was a plague they could catch from me. I understood. They were cowards.

The Diary of John Winthrop

Governor of The Massachussetts Bay Colony

S eptember 30, 1630.
   Wolves killed six calves at Salem and they killed one wolf. Thomas Morton, of Merrymount, was judged to be imprisoned until he could be sent back to England for his many injuries offered to the Indians, and other misdemeanors. The Master of the *Gifte* refused to carry him. Finch, of Watertown, had his wigwam burnt and all his goods. Billington executed at Plymouth for murdering one. Mr. Phillips, the minister at Watertown, and others had their hay burnt. The wolves killed some swine at Saugus. A cow died at Plymouth and a goat at Boston from eating Indian corn.

Alice Bradford

On the evening Billington was hanged, my husband climbed into bed and spoke of the colony's business. A cow had died that morning due to tainted corn. More loss of profit befell us. I thought it must have been heavy on his conscience—what responsibility the colony had now to care for Eleanor Billington, the widow. But I was not exactly correct.

We'll have to scrub the blood off his land, William said.

Clean it? I asked, like a child.

Remove them.

Excise them from the colony?

He was agitated.

Remove Billingtons as landholders. Put the care to someone else.

I sat up taller.

But where will Eleanor live? And Francis?

William moved away from me.

I've extended my duty as governor far beyond what other governors view is most charitable.

My husband quoted Psalm 7:15. *Good Wife, he hath made a pit and digged it, and is fallen into the pit he made.*

Prithee, reconsider, I said, in a voice too firm, I see that now.

There was a silence, a long silence, though hardly any time passed until what happened next. I did not see the hand move with force through the air, but I felt it on my cheek. My head knocked back against the wall and my body, too. I was the one flung against the wall this time, not some ill-bred neighbor. What would the newcomers think? I hoped the children, too, were sleeping deeply.

William the younger called for me.

John asked, from across the room, *All right?*

Fine, I said. *Just dropped something.*

It was plain that was not what had happened.

William leaned in close to me and whispered, *It seems, Good Wife, you wish to be the husband.*

I had misstepped. I first thought, *I shall not do that again.*

I second thought, *Did Dorothy know this William, too?*

In the silence, Mercy screamed.

Before I went to her I said to William, *I am sorry. I trust in you.*

When I returned to bed, William was kneeling on the floor, his head and hands in prayer. It was a silent prayer. I lay there. When he was through he did not reach for me.

But I woke in the night to William's touch. As sweetly as he had ever been, with softness and the kindest hands he cupped my cheek and looked me in the eyes. There was apology there.

He kissed me.

You do not understand the weight upon me, William said.

So recent in fear of him, but he was correct, I did not understand fully, and I wanted to give him this, my understanding.

I lifted his linen. He lifted up my night dress. Our chests bare to one another, then pressed warm against the evening chill. We fell asleep warmed in this way. But in the morning I woke to the cold metal of his gun betwixt us.

Dorothy

He had no gun in Holland but when we were on the ship he had a gun and he slept with it betwixt us.

Yesterday we saw land but I saw all that there was not: no church, no home, no friends to comfort.

He said, *Look around. We are a community. We rely on one another. God's providence is here. I feel it. Rest with our brethren. I will be back before nightfall.*

He kissed the top of my head. I wished he had kissed my mouth.

My husband aboard a shallop of men, his musket high above him. I watched him row away from me. He was a man now of a different sort—was it hunger, necessity, greed?

I went back to the tween deck. I made dinner and ate it.

The next morning, he had not returned. Us women sleeping, except I. I walked past the More children: Ellen, eight years old, Richard, six, and Mary, four. Their bodies tangled together in love and comfort. One brother, Jasper, seven years old and two days dead. A prayer had been said and two seamen rolled him off the deck.

I pushed my tongue to the roof of my mouth. My two front teeth slid forward. In my hands were my gloves. I slipped them beside Ellen. She would need them, and so much more, in the new colony.

I climbed up the ladder and went to the back of the ship.

I am on the deck, remembering. My dearest consort, Alice, cajoling me to get up from the hay and pick tulips with her. Her laughter, her loping, and her belief.

My mother, warning me, after a bad dream as a child, that no one knows who is chosen, that it might not be me, that outward signs of my goodliness might suggest I was. But I tipped over chairs and told lies anyway.

Out on the deck where I am not permitted to be. Something cool and wet inside my ear. I place my finger there. Blood.

My husband on land. I hope he is safe. I hope our John is, too.

The edge of the ship slicked by cold air and ocean. To stand on the deck and hear the cries of dolphins. To lean off the rail and watch the waves.

An animal arcs across the water. A whale!

A creature William laments he does not have the equipment to kill. *All that oil.* He means all that profit.

Not a good enough mother, not a good enough wife. My fingers on the railing, staying there until I can no longer feel them.

Good Wife, he calls me.

In death, he'll call me not.

No, do not think thus, it is the seamen's illness, making old wounds of the body and of the spirit reemerge.

To break and spread over the sea. Not carried in a casket, not brought back up to the ship.

To act, just to act. That is the glorious thing—

A foot slips and I let it?

If ever I beheld love, John, there was thee. A better mother there will be.

Alice Bradford

The face we wear by day is not the face that appears at night, nor on a vessel seven weeks at sea.

Perhaps she suffered it all privately. She wore her dignified, Christian face at the final wave goodbye to her husband. She walked erect back down to the tween deck, and the next morning she jumped off a ship three stories high, into the November ocean, without celebration or warning.

The night before, she cooked dinner for herself and the very pregnant Susanna, who had trouble bending over to the fire. She put other mothers' sons to sleep, she gave no sign, the women said, of what was to come. This is how they knew it was an accident.

But in my solemnest of moments, in my prideful moments, I like to think I could have saved her. That I could have noticed in her eyes what we had wondered about in that man on the bridge. In my vainest of moments, I like to think I would have seen the light bend toward an irretrievable darkness, and turned it elsewhere.

Eleanor Billington

H e's dead and buried. I go there and spit on it, I do. *Fool*, I say.

Homes are cold dark places when those you love are dead.

I have two graves I visit.

I have firewood, a house, two graves, and a storehouse of food, far more than what Francis and I need.

I do not have my mother, I do not have my son, I do not have my husband.

His body was brought to me that afternoon, purple at the rope line, bluing at his face.

I prayed over him for heaven where the preacher prayed for hell.

My husband killed one man, 'tis true. But Standish killed a dozen, slaughtered men with the knives around their own necks, chased a boy out of the wetu and hanged him from an elm. These *elders* proudly display the heads of those they've murdered, wave the dead men's clothes like flags, and say it is for our safety.

Crimes happen every day. Some brag of them and are called heroes. The wealthy who beat their servants cite Scripture and are pardoned. Recently, a husband and wife beat their young boy servant and forced him out in winter to mend fences. He died in the snow. He was found with black toes, bed sores, and urine up and down his legs. Bruises and open sores on his chest. Years of beatings. Twelve years old. Were those two hanged? Nay, not with their pockets. No, they were pardoned, paid off just like the bishops who gave alms back in England, which the puritans were so set against removing, saying *How corrupt, how corrupt.* But they are no different.

Alice Bradford

On the day after Master Billington's execution, I had a headache, which made it difficult to see my way down the hill. Susanna, Elizabeth, and I gathered our children and went to the dock to wave the *Gifte* off. The Master of the ship had deemed the weather favorable enough to depart but I suspected he was waiting until the verdict was given, and the hanging done, not being one to miss the entertainment, but also wanting to depart swiftly from the crime.

On the way down the hill, we women discussed the execution. Now that he was dead, we spoke more freely of the Billingtons.

They weren't right, Elizabeth said. *The whole lot of them. You could see they would cause trouble.*

They signed up for seven years of servitude, Susanna said. *I doubt they gave us one single year.*

We all agreed. Profane. From London. Who knew what friends they consorted with? Never knew God.

The least godly creatures God has made, someone said. It may have been I.

From soil to sand we went, through a scraggly line of trees, shallowly rooted to the sand.

I scanned the faces for Eleanor, feeling dread that our paths might cross. There was no escaping one another. I would see her at the meetinghouse, the brook, the ovens, the fields. I wanted to delay facing her, though.

A crowd was gathered to see the ship off. Susanna clutched my arm. I knew what she was thinking. Our servants could turn on us. All of them. At any moment. There were more of them than us. It was important not to remind them of this. It was important to bring them to the church. We musn't let them see how afraid we were.

Susanna, I said, and pulled her hand away.

I whispered, *They are watching. We mustn't be afraid.*

And was that them snarling at us?

Hold your chin high. We've done nothing wrong.

Susanna adjusted her posture.

The first in line to board the ship was Thomas Weston.

He said the only positive thing that could be said about what he witnessed in our colony.

The Good Wives serve ye well and blessed be they who have such bounty nearby. May God's light always shine upon you.

Thomas Weston knew what words to speak, but there was not feeling beneath it. Behind him were three newcomers. One couple, one single man. All of whom had intended to make our colony their home. But now they were sending us their apologies. The single man gave an excuse: *My mother's ill*, but the couple, when I wished them well, barely smiled. I pressed biscuits into their hands.

It would be good to be unburdened by more bodies to feed, but it was not good for the spirit to know that they did not wish to be among us.

But the threat is gone! I wanted to say. *Now we can live as God intended!*

What a fool I was back then, thinking the death of one person could end the lasciviousness of others.

A seaman placed a coin on the starboard side. The sails were ready, the anchor was up, and the passengers were below in the tween deck. We said prayers for them, hoped God would grant them a swift, safe journey back to London. I hated to see a ship off, even if those aboard would have given us difficulty. I hoped the ones who had stayed feared God and the gallows. But it proved not to be so.

❦

The sounds of the wilderness had always been among us, but now they appeared more sinister. While tending livestock, making candles, baking, knitting, or weaving, through the oak groves I would hear a sound and wonder, was that a bear or was that a man set against us?

At night the mastiffs and spaniels of our community, each separated in our homes and gardens, called to one another. A lonely call, wanting at night their friends of day. I heard this as I lay in bed, unable to sleep, listening to the breath of my husband and children, and at the community's edge, the lurking wolves.

William installed a lock upon our door. Susanna's wreath came down, taken off by her husband, and instead on the door he put two latches. We looked at those who did not attend church with more and more suspicion. Danger was everywhere, we learned, and sometimes the grandest threat was within your own community.

Part Three

Eleanor Billington

Six years have passed since my husband's execution. I'm a fifty-three-year-old woman and do you know what they have done to me of recent?

There was a man, John Doane, who looked on me with lewd eyes when no one watched and scornful eyes when someone did. A church deacon he was, no different from the rest, wanted power. Took it where he could. Making his hand linger at my arm when I passed him. I told Alice and all who'd listen he was vile.

She said, *Be careful, Eleanor.*

Slander is what she warned of. She was wrong, but if there was any benevolence in a Bradford, it was in her and not her husband.

I called it as I saw it. For speaking the truth, I tell ye, the truth about my neighbor. John Doane, as I said, was looking for any opening to put his seed into. He set his eyes upon me, a widow, living alone. All I had to protect myself was my mouth. So I spoketh.

I shall tell it how it happened. One evening I was milking, and John Doane came to me and offered me abuse by putting his hand under my petticoat. I turned aside with much ado, saved myself, and when I was settled to milking again he took me by the shoulder and pulled me nearly backward. I clapped one hand on the ground and held fast to the cow's teat with the other hand and cried out as loud as I have ever yelled. I did not think at fifty-three I would be fending off men as if I was a young milkmaid. A servant boy, Abbott, heard me. Doane told the boy to go on about his business. I bade the lad to stay. The lad remained, but all the while Doane chastised him for obeying a woman.

In the morning I went to Standish to report what Doane had done.

Slander, Standish accused *me* thus.

He and Bradford called a trial of *me* and *I* was convicted.

I was ordered to be stripped from the waist up, even my linens, my wrists tied to the back of an oxen-drawn cart and whipped through town.

On the cold morning in early June of my punishment, Myles Standish reached toward me, tried to lift off my linen. I grabbed it back.

That's only for me and my late husband to do, I said.

The crowd chuckled. They didn't deserve my merry-making.

I took off my clothes. Oh, how those hypocrites watched.

My breasts were bare and my nipples were so cold and erect they stung, as if from a suckling infant with newly emerging teeth. I was aware of them, flopping by the weight and the men—and some women, too—watching them. I've always had a nice bosom.

Myles Standish cracked his whip behind me and ordered the oxen to start walking. He snapped it a few times in the air to entice the crowd.

The whip lashed against my back. I gritted my teeth.

I'll have you remember! I called to them. *It was I that wiped ye faces and ye arses that first winter. Half ye's died!*

I knew this was the only time—unless whipped again— that I would have this much of the colony's attention. I had to make the most of it.

Your brethren dragged the dying into the woods and propped them up against trees, with muskets by their side. Concerned, so concerned they were, for themselves more than the dying. But not us Billingtons. We cared for them. Your governor wanted the Indians to see a forest sentinel to save himself. I'll have ye remember there would have been more dead without us. We Billingtons did not drag the dying bodies into the forest. I cared for ye!

I looked out on that crowd. They were unmoved. Why did their faces smile? Then I realized. Only three of the women here had been on the *Mayflower*. Only a handful of men. This crowd was a crowd of strangers. They didn't remember what I had done for them, they didn't know, they did not care. To them, I was the widow of the first murderer.

I kept talking because I had to keep walking and it helped to draw my attention away from the pain. The whip turned, singed. He'd broken skin. I felt blood slide down my back as if it were thick sweat. I would not cry out. The onlookers were confused, or uninterested by my speech, enthralled instead by my naked body. Nothing I could say meant anything to these strangers.

I, a widow, fifty-three years of age. I, a woman, with every right to speak the truth.

The old bloody linen and bird-pecked skull moved in the wind above us.

Get a look, I said.

That's what they had come for, those hypocrites, to see a naked woman's body beat into submission. I shan't be beaten down in spirit, only in body can they scar me.

John Doane was there, happy to see what I had denied him. The hypocrites gave him the view he wanted all along. Some men enjoy it, seeing us women bare-breasted and whipped—it is what they would to do to us if they could.

Bradford leaned against a house rather than do the whipping himself, as if I might not notice him and recall that it was he who had issued the punishment.

When it was all over, I returned home to discover they had impounded my trespassing heifer, who had escaped beyond the fence while I was away.

The next day, the young Johnson father, whom my husband had helped, brought me milk still warm from his heifer.

Alice Bradford

My husband's comfort, in his final years, was Hebrew. Many of our friends had left Plymouth by then. Susanna and Edward built an estate in Marshfield. Captain Standish lived in Duxbury. But us? Though we had the means, we never left the house in Plymouth that William built, just added more rooms.

Nightly, my husband lamented: *Their appetite for land has caused the town, like a mother grown old, to be forsaken by her children. Not in affection but bodily presence . . . it will be the ruin of New England . . . and will provoke the Lord's displeasure against them.*

I told him to rest. I told him it would be as God intended.

He tested his life's work and teachings to God's original language. To get as close as he could to God's words, he learned Hebrew. After thirty years as governor, he was a child again, learning language, and delighted in what he could recall, and agitated at what phrases he could not hold together. Sometimes, he wrote poetry that spoketh of God making this banquet in the wilderness for us. But my husband disputed over riverways with Dutch companies, both parties presenting Indian deeds they claimed were granted to them. Eight years after Billington's punishment, Governor Winthrop asked for my husband's help in securing safety for colonists to the north and soldiers my husband did send. The Lord blessed their endeavors. They slew or took in seven hundred Pequot Indians. The men not slain would not endure the yoke and were sold by Governor Winthrop to investors in Bermuda in exchange for African slaves, as were the male children. The women and girls were disposed about in the towns. Those that arrived to be our lifelong servants appeared so terrified that it was a fright to receive them.

That same year, it pleased God to bless Plymouth with several healthy calves, but also that year there was a fretful earthquake, heard before it was felt. What gave God such displeasure? The world rumbled, coming northward, which caused the platters and dishes that stood upon our shelves to clatter and fall down, and caused I myself to fall. People were afraid of the houses themselves. But my husband said henceforth that the summers were not so hot after the earthquake and therefore quite favorable for the growth of our corn.

One morning, William woke from bed, as the sun was cresting above the sea line. He turned to me, lighter in spirit than I had seen in months. He ran his hand along my thigh, upward.

Good Husband, I said. It had been years.

He found his way betwixt my linen slip, and placed his middle finger at the source of all my body's tingling. He circled his finger there.

My husband said, *I have just seen the entertainments of Paradise.*

I bid him to stop what pleasure he was wishing to give me. So near it seemed he was, to the end, and so oddly joyous now. *Is this profane?* I wondered, but did not speak it. My husband continued.

We lay there, together, him and I. If these were his final moments, this was not the deathbed scene I would tell our children, our townsfolk, or the colony.

He closed his eyes and kept them that way. I closed my own.

Here we were. He was sixty-seven.

I let out little puffs of breath.

He said, *My dove in the clefts of the rock.*

I turned and kissed him and thought of that first time, on the shores of Plymouth.

The days tending to his care had left me more tired than I'd let myself realize. I had forgotten what pleasure could feel like.

Afterward, we both drifted asleep. When I woke, his hand was still betwixt my legs, but it was cold. I startled upright. I thought him dead. But he was not yet dead. God granted him two more weeks.

The final hours of a man reveal him.

On the ninth of May, in the year of our Lord sixteen hundred and fifty-seven, at sixty-seven years of age, my husband, William Bradford, said, *I have heard God. He promises happiness in another world.*

He said: *Farewell, dear wife. I love thee. Your better husband is above.*

To heaven he went, our dearest country. We buried him on the summit of Burial Hill in sight of the sand hills of Cape Cod.

Eleanor Billington

J ust me and Francis here in Plymouth. I tried to send him north to find his place away from these puritans, but he is as oxen as his father. He finds himself in court too often.

The raised skin on my back is smooth now, thin like pine roots, but pinker than the rest of me.

Governor Bradford has written quite the story, borrowed from myth, it is, *Of Plymouth Plantation*. A failed colony his was, but preserved in his writing as he wished it would have been. More lies than truth, just like the man. It was Tom Morton who spoketh the truth: my husband, beloved by many, wronged by the leaders of Plymouth.

We gave them our best bodies. We gave them our workhorse years. And what did they give us? Murder. Banishment. Starvation. Revoking on what was rightfully ours. My husband killed a man, yes, it is true, but that land was ours.

Once, being a Billington was a mark of bravery. It was my husband who found the first brook here, my husband who was brave enough to see first what was beyond the forest's edge, and my son who found the lake. Now, even in colonies farther north and south—in Massachusetts Bay, in New Netherlands—they think of Plymouth as cruel and unpredictable.

A place in God's favor? Ha. They've made again what they claimed they wished to leave. They have the indentured English, but also Indians they've coerced or forced into servitude. The only difference is they are the ones in power. They are the ones to blame.

Go on, I told Francis. *Leave me in this rotting corpse of a colony. There is nothing here for you.*

When he tried to be kind and stay, I was mean to him. This was the only way for him to outlive his lineage. I insulted him to make sure he dothn't come back. But back he came, and finds himself in court for not attending town meetings and sundry other petty accusations.

Alice Bradford

I t's September again. The sun shines through dying leaves. My second husband gone twelve years, my first husband gone thirty-five. At the end of life, everything comes back to you as if happening today. What does it mean? Why did it happen? The revelation never comes. Instead there is my granddaughter, the sound of her feet running down the hall and small, daily illuminations.

There are seventy thousand English settlers living in one hundred and ten towns in this area. Three thousand people in ours. *What if we would have landed farther north?* I sometimes wonder. Boston thrives as it was easy to see, even in the year of our Lord sixteen hundred and thirty, it would—a big, deep port for ships, lusher land, and larger rivers.

Our one-room cottage has become the largest home in the colony, with seven rooms. My bed is veiled in a white curtain. Such privacy I have now, for dying. Privacy now when it matters little to me, except to shield my grand-daughter from death. Elizabeth runs into my room in the mornings, saying, *It is morning time, Grandmum.* She likes to run her hands along the parchment of my skin. When I look into her eyes I know how fast the world is, how fast a life is. I pray for her a long one.

Our own little colony upon a downward slope is slowly sliding into the sea. So much that happens, happens imper-ceptibly. All creatures speak to one another, though so soft we cannot hear. The sound a ground mole makes to another cannot be heard by the human ear, but I am certain it exists.

The first spring flowers emerge, crack open, fall apart.

There is rarely a Sabbath I do not walk by the meeting-house and find someone in the stocks. Drunkenness, adul-tery, fornication before or without contract, slanderous speech, cursing—these are the most common crimes.

The surviving orphan from the *Mayflower,* Richard More, lives. He is a seaman, but more famously, a drunkard, and when he visits the meetinghouse sweating off yester-day's wine, when the women see him lingering amongst the vegetables in their gardens, the generation that is still here to recall what he lost—his mother and his siblings—grant him some forgiveness. Those who know his story treat him more forgivingly than perhaps they should.

We have made more laws. It does not seem to stop the crimes. Following the murder of Newcomen came accu-sations upon accusations.

Widow Warren brought her servant Thomas Williams to court for refusing to perform his duties. According to Thomas, Widow Warren gave him chores that required him to be out in the elements in the coldest days of winter. Chopping wood beyond necessity, mending fences, and the like. To his protest Widow Warren said, *Thomas, fear God and do your duty*. But Thomas Williams, worked up into a passion and distemper, replied, *I fear neither God nor the devil*. Widow Warren charged him with blasphemy. Thomas claimed a momentary lapse due to an imbalance of humors, but the governor did not agree, and he was sentenced to ten lashes in the public square.

I sometimes wonder if it has made things worse, the lawmaking and the punishments, giving them even more ideas—how to fornicate and abuse both people and animals. One young man who tried to quell his lust with cows, a horse, and three goats was hanged and the animals were slaughtered. All that death, and all of that costly meat, which of course, in keeping with the Bible, no one ate.

Buggery and sundry variations of other carriages have occurred. Women whipped and walked around the town by the elders as punishment. Good Wife Norman was found in a bed in lewd behavior with Mary Hamon. There is no law for this betwixt women. Good Wife confessed publicly and Mary, a single woman, was released. She has not been seen in Plymouth since. Men found lying together are hanged. But for women, a public confession is often enough. I see Good Wife Norman on Sundays in church. The confession righted her position in the community. I oft wonder if it relieved her, the revelation of a secret.

I recall the days of youth, dreaming on the hillside with Dorothy. Her hair falling down in front of her face. Her standing over me, singing a song of the poplar trees. The summer our bosoms needed support but did not yet have it. The morning we lifted off our linens and she turned to me. Sunlight through the flowers. Her breasts, firm as two bowls, where mine already began to drift. I went to her. We laced our hands together. Our bosoms touching.

Let's practice, she said. *For our husbands.*

And so we did.

❧

From my home in the center of town, I often smell the rotting corpses of wolves. Their heads are nailed to the side of the meetinghouse. Each man receives a bounty for trapping them. Wolves kill cattle and swine nearly every day.

With more from Europe arriving to this coast, men hasten to claim land as their own. A year after Billington's trial, we had a minister, Roger Williams, that questioned how it was we came to reside upon this land and the land of our trading posts in Bourne and Kennebec—though the King's signature was on our charter—and did we not owe the Indians? My husband promptly asked him to leave the colony. Indians do live amongst us. Fewer are the English indentured and more are the Indians, some as lifelong servants. But there is talk of unrest. The elders discuss the need for new laws to disallow the Indians from owning firearms, to disallow them from using their English Masters' guns to hunt for their Masters' fowl.

Our fur business in Kennebec is declining. The beavers have nearly disappeared—too many caught in too short of a time, or, perhaps, they have moved farther away from us. The colonists' swine still trample on the Wampanoag's crops, though now the Plymouth court has determined that it is the responsibility of the Wampanoag Indians to erect fences, if so it is the livestock do bother them. Most recently, the younger Plymouth men—my Constant amongst them—developed a deed granting themselves land at Pocasset.

What we value was worn away by relations with nonbelievers. Our children are intermarrying, here, as well, but instead of becoming too Dutch, as we feared when we lived in Holland, they are losing sight of God's plan by the lure of Boston merchants and Quaker women.

John left this way, twenty-odd years ago, when he married Martha Bourne, and moved to Norwich. Though I like to think I was a mother to him, I confess it was not the same as with my own. God has not granted them any children.

The ones I bore myself stayed close. William the younger married Alice, who begot me ten grandchildren. Mercy, my only daughter, married Benjamin Vermayes in December of the year of our Lord sixteen hundred and forty-eight, but God saw it fit to take her before He did my husband, and without the gift of children. My youngest, Joseph, lives here with me, in this house his father built. He has one daughter and another coming. His wife, Jeal, is a comfort. I like to hear her in the mornings singing to my granddaughter.

Table scraps of what people once said to me come, unbidden. I am in my memories more these days than out in the field, my past more vivid than the present. Most mornings, I wake before the cockles' crow. My thoughts are fast then and full of everything I wish I could take back.

I am forty again, laundering, my children kicking around my feet. A burden it felt, all those requests to be picked up when there were so many tasks to do. What I would give now though, to do it all again, to hear my daughter, two years old, say, *Mum, please.*

But I took time with them as I could. I stared into their eyes. And they grew strong and respectable and godly.

These are the memories I wish to have.

But there are others.

The next generation doth not remember what we sacrificed. In other communities, like Salem, the girls are defying their mothers, refusing to wipe the tables clean, laughing merrily while reading poetry but claiming illness when their mothers bring out the Bible.

Not our girls, I say. Not our girls. But one day I fear, it might be.

This is the way of generations, to remember a better time. Just as our parents thought we were losing our English manners in Holland and now we think this of our children. Even their voices are losing the inflections of our homeland. I have warned them, often, of retaining their English customs. The good ones, at least.

Nowadays, I must climb up to Burial Hill to visit my friends. The cemetery has the best view in Plymouth. We lost Elizabeth first, to illness in the year of our Lord sixteen hundred and forty. Susanna, fourteen years later. She and Edward had built a large estate they named Careswell when they were younger, but in the year of our Lord sixteen hundred and forty-six, Edward was called for by Oliver Cromwell to London. Edward had a portrait of himself done there and sent it back to Plymouth. In the portrait, he holds a letter signed: *Your loving wife, Susanna.* By the time the portrait arrived to Plymouth, Edward was a commissioner with the Royal Navy on a mission to gain control of Jamaica from the Spanish and his wife, Susanna, had left us for the Lord.

My will is written. *I, Alice Bradford, being weak in body, but of disposing mind, do make and ordain this my last will and testament.* Soon, I, too, will be buried. But my body will lie at the foot of my husband's grave. Wills are like wedding vows, are they not? Prescriptive in phrase, but no less meaningful for it. Soon after Master Billington's departure, my husband surprised me with a green gown to match the color of my eyes, which it pleased me to wear on special occasions—my children's wedding celebrations and a few necessary gatherings of elders and wives in Salem.

I promised the gown to Jeal. She is a plain-spoken woman and will wear it with dignity and without pride. The bed that was Dorothy's mother's, the one I now lie on, will go to my sister. I will give my eldest son, Constant Southworth, the heifers, a young mare, and the land at Paomet. To my youngest, Joseph, I will give one half of my sheep, the other half to Constant. To my middle, Captain William, the white oxen and the white heifer. The books, one hundred and fifty of them, will go to my friend Thomas Prence who was governor betwixt my husband's long appointments, and a comfort in my widowed years. To my granddaughter Elizabeth, the only child of my deceased Thomas, I will give seven pounds. For my servant Mary, a calf, delivered to her next spring if I decease this winter, and next winter if I decease this fall.

All the remaining sundry are to be divided among Constant, William, and Joseph. John was given land by his father when he passed and I do not think to trouble him with a journey back to Plymouth for any of my affairs. When last I saw him, at his father's funeral, I gave him his mother's painting. For most of my life, I had my dearest consort's bowls, her son, and her husband, but I did not have her. *It is not right*, William would say, *to keep loss this close.* But if I let go of grief, I let go of her. To be no longer grieving is to no longer have her with me.

I gave my husband's book *Of Plymouth Plantation* to the care of Joseph. I wish to keep it close to me, for to do so is to keep William here, as well. Sometimes I enter the study and open it. *In our hearts, we were pilgrims.* Even though he has long since passed on to heaven, I am careful to return the book as I found it.

We longed for a better future in God's favor, but in many ways, the colony my husband planned for was not a success. We live among the Anglican, as if we lived again with those who believed against us, who sided with those who punished us in England. When we left Holland, the truce between the Dutch and the Spanish was nearly ending, and here, the treaty made between my husband and the great sachem is ending—both men have perished. Some here want more and more, not stopping at God's good grace. I feel tension growing. In many ways, our better future is an imagined past.

But my husband's life—and what he left to me and our children—was far more prosperous than it would have been had he remained a fustian weaver in Holland.

Behind the house, at the edge of the garden, I have placed one of Dorothy's bowls, deep in the earth's soil, deeper than I hope she or he who lives here next will seek. I have placed her there so she can smell the lavender. I hope she soars high up with God. Perhaps we will meet again up there, if He deems it so.

The head has been taken down from the post above the meetinghouse, but the linen with Wituwamat's blood still waves.

AUTHOR'S NOTE

I was first drawn to this story by the female experiences left out from accounts by early seventeenth-century colonists in America. Particularly, I was intrigued by the knowledge that William Bradford, who wrote the history of the *Mayflower* passengers in his book *Of Plymouth Plantation*, scantly mentions the death of his first wife, Dorothy. Much later, another writer who was not on the ship writes that Dorothy slipped off of the *Mayflower*, which was moored, in what is now Provincetown Harbor. Why didn't Bradford mention the cause of his first wife's death? Is it possible her death was not an accident? These questions led me down various paths for a number of years until I was able to imagine the voice of Dorothy's close friend, Alice. Finally, while in London one summer, Eleanor's voice came to me; the story of a fed-up indentured servant, economically and socially disadvantaged in this new colony, who represented an experience that I hadn't seen enough of. Was the Billington family a collection of troublemakers, as the leader of Plymouth described, or were their actions indicative of nascent unrest in the colony?

In telling this story, I wanted to add more possibilities to our collective imagination about "the pilgrims." I also wanted to challenge certain myths, such as the belief that all the *Mayflower* passengers were seeking freedom to practice their religion. The separatists living in Holland *were* already able to practice their religion. What else motivated them? The people on the *Mayflower* arrived to Patuxet from a variety of backgrounds and for different reasons—indentured servants who signed up out of various necessities, craftsmen hired to assist in the physical creation of the colony, people looking for economic gain, one soldier paid to protect the settlers, and a set of children sent away by their father without their mother's knowledge. The *Mayflower*, in fact, was the ship organized to carry the non-separatists across the ocean. But when the *Speedwell* was abandoned in England, perhaps due to leaks, or perhaps because the captain did not wish to make the journey, the separatist puritans added themselves to the *Mayflower*.

Though this is a work of fiction, I have tried to take care with depictions of people real and imagined in and around Patuxet, the place later named Plymouth. This novel takes place mostly within the palisade of Plymouth and aims to investigate factions within the "pilgrim" community, therefore the novel is primarily told from the point of view of the English. The stories of the Indigenous people of the Wampanoag Nation were a part of my research, though, and I am grateful to a member of the Wampanoag Nation, who asked not to be named, for her invaluable assistance in this aspect of the novel.

I am also grateful for the help of several scholars, particularly my correspondence with David Silverman, who was kind enough to share an advance copy of his new book, *This Land Is Their Land* (Bloomsbury, 2019), with me. Thank you to numerous people who responded to my email inquiries, offering various (and oftentimes contradictory!) perspectives: Clark Davis, Lisa Brooks, Peg Baker, James Baker, Jeremy Bangs, and Cynthia Tinney, among many others. Thank you to Kimberly Toney at the American Antiquarian Society, who drew my attention to the Foster Map, her curation "From English to Algonquian," and several other primary documents, including multiple execution sermons, as well as Elizabeth Pope, Ashley Cataldo, and Nan Wolverton, who offered various materials from the stacks that further illuminated this novel. I'm thankful for several critical books including, but not limited to: Martha L. Finch's *Dissenting Bodies: Corporealities in Early New England*, David Silverman's *Thundersticks*, Lisa Brooks's *Our Beloved Kin*, and Amy E. Den Ouden's *Beyond Conquest: Native Peoples and the Struggle for History in New England*, as well as several primary documents including Plymouth court records and estate listings, letters, Amsterdam court records, *New England's Prospect* by William Wood, William Bradford's *Of Plymouth Plantation*, John Smith's *The General History of New England*, Thomas Morton's *The New English Canaan*, and Edward Winslow's *Good News from New England*. I am also appreciative of the resources and materials from Plymouth Hall Museum, the Plymouth Colony Archive Project, and the Plimoth Plantation living history museum. All of the above have contributed to the imaginative development of this novel.

A challenge in writing this novel was how to retain the terminology used in 1630 though it is not the language of today. Alice, for instance, sometimes uses the offensive term "Savages" for Indigenous people of the Northeast Woodlands, as her husband did at times. For Eleanor, I've chosen "Indian" or named the tribal affiliation specifically, to align with the sentiment of Thomas Morton, who oversaw the trading post at Merrymount, before he was banished, and who wrote *The New English Canaan*. One other note: the English settlers often did not call people by their correct names. For instance, they either mistakenly thought the Wampanoag massasoit Ousamequin was named Massasoit, or they rejected his name because "Massasoit" was deemed easier to say than his actual name. But "Massasoit" is a title rather than a name. Instead, his name was Ousamequin and would be translated as "Yellow Feather" in English. According to the member of the Wampanoag Nation I consulted with, the Wampanoag Nation had over sixty-nine sachem districts with several villages within each district and the massasoit was the sachem chosen as the nation's spokesperson. Similarly, "Squanto" is the incorrect name for the Wampanoag man who spoke English and acted as a translator between the Wampanoag people and the English settlers: His name was Tisquantum.

One might wonder why I do not use the term "pilgrim" much in the novel. The term "pilgrim" is a general term that suggests one who travels and is used only briefly in William Bradford's account. More specifically, I am attempting to show the social space of the time and therefore Eleanor Billington uses the pejorative term "puritan." The terms "Puritan" and "puritan"—the capitalization was initially inconsistent—is first noted in the 1560s, appearing as a term against those Protestants who wanted more church reforms to Queen Elizabeth's 1559 Religious Settlement. The term was not used by any religious group to describe their own affiliations. Rather, it was a term more closely aligned with "stickler" and "hypocrite," as Eleanor uses it. Unlike other religious groups of the time, including Calvinists, Catholics, or Lutherans, puritans were not clearly defined, nor did they self-identify as puritans. Instead, they were part of various churches and not even aligned in their desire for particular reformations. "Puritan" was a term used by their enemies. More accurately, we would call the Plymouth elders Separatist Puritans or separatists, because they wanted reform within the church but chose to separate rather than further trying to purify from within, but these were not terms used at the time.

Exploring these stories necessitated—and, thankfully, welcomed—fiction. These fabrications are numerous and include the compression of time and the creation of composite characters. However, each character in the novel was a real person and the murder and the trial really did take place.

ACKNOWLEDGMENTS

Thank you, Julie Barer, for believing in me and my writing continuously and insisting on the best. With gratitude to my editor, Nancy Miller, for asking the right questions to push my thinking. Your suggestions are steadfastly gentle but transformative. Thank you. Thank you to The Book Group and Bloomsbury people who have done amazing things for my books—Gleni Bartels, Marie Coolman, Nicole Cunningham, Elizabeth Ellis, Nicole Jarvis, Laura Keefe, Liese Mayer, Laura Phillips, Patti Ratchford, Valentina Rice, and many others.

Thank you to Olaf Haje for the artwork. Thank you to my early readers and dear friends Anton DiSclafani and Shena McAuliffe.

With gratitude to my friends and colleagues at Miami University for the conversations—Cathy Wagner, Mike Hatch, Michele Navakas, cris cheek, Margaret Luongo, Daisy Hernández, Madelyn Detloff, Theresa Kulbaga, Kaara

Peterson, Jody Bates, Brian Roley, Keith Tuma, Anita Mannur, and Erik Jensen, as well as the English Department for the semester-long and summer research support. Thank you to John Altman, Tim Melley, and the Altman Fellowship program for bringing together scholars from various disciplines for the year-long conversation about truth. Thank you to my students past and present—you challenge and inspire me with your stories, curiosities, insights, and compassion.

Thank you to my friends and mentors at the University of Denver, who encouraged this project when I was just beginning it as a doctoral student. With gratitude to Brian Kitely, Laird Hunt, Clark Davis, Joanna Ruocco, Adam Rovner, Nichol Weizenbeck, and Susan Schulten.

Thank you to the communities of people who love and support those whom I love and support, which enables me to escape into imaginary worlds for a while, while also being a mother.

Thank you to my parents, and grandparents, and great-grandparents.

Thank you to my two youngest teachers, Inez and Arthur.

Thank you, Jerritt, for your discernment, love, humor, support, and belief.

Thank you, dear reader, for meeting me here.

A NOTE ON THE AUTHOR

TaraShea Nesbit is the author of the novel *The Wives of Los Alamos*, which was a finalist for the PEN/Robert W. Bingham Prize, a *New York Times Book Review* "Editors' Choice," a *Library Journal* "Best Debut," the winner of two New Mexico–Arizona Book Awards, and published in four languages. She has been awarded a creative writing fellowship at the American Antiquarian Society for her second novel, as well as granted an Individual Excellence Award from the Ohio Arts Council for her essays, which have been published in *Granta, Ninth Letter, Fourth Genre,* and *Salon.* She earned a PhD in literature and creative writing from the University of Denver, with a focus on prose, and an MFA from Washington University in St. Louis, with a focus on poetry. She is an associate professor at Miami University and lives in Oxford, Ohio, with her family.